"What do you have in mind to do with the house?" Ted asked.

Fiona pointed up the stairs. "My living quarters will be up there. The old parlor will make a perfect waiting room, and I'll partition the other rooms to be an exam room, an office, and maybe space for birthing classes, if there's a demand for them," she said.

"I wouldn't be surprised if there was," Ted said. "Plenty of Amish women prefer home births. You should be able to build a good practice, if you stay."

"If?" Her eyebrows shot up. "I'm not going through all this trouble with the intent of leaving. I'm not going anywhere." She stroked the intricate carving of the newel post. "This is home."

Her voice trembled with emotion on the last word, touching him. It made him want to know what lay behind that emotion. But he didn't figure he had the right. Not yet.

Books by Marta Perry

MARTA PERRY

has written everything, including Sunday school curriculum, travel articles and magazine stories, in twenty years of writing, but she feels she's found her home in the stories she writes for Love Inspired.

Marta lives in rural Pennsylvania, but she and her husband spend part of each year at their second home in South Carolina. When she's not writing, she's probably visiting her children and her beautiful grandchildren, traveling or relaxing with a good book.

Marta loves hearing from readers and she'll write back with a signed bookplate or bookmark. Write to her c/o Steeple Hill Books, 233 Broadway, Suite 1001, New York, NY 10279, e-mail her at marta@martaperry.com, or visit her on the Web at www.martaperry.com.

Restless Hearts
Marta Perry

1 800 309 0355 (handwritten)

Steeple
Hill®

Published by Steeple Hill Books™

STEEPLE HILL BOOKS

Steeple
Hill®

ISBN-13: 978-0-373-87424-8
ISBN-10:   0-373-87424-3

RESTLESS HEARTS

www.SteepleHill.com

Printed in U.S.A.

And we know that in all things,
God works for the good of those who love him,
who have been called according to His purpose.
—*Romans* 8:28

This story is dedicated to my granddaughter, Estella Terese Johnson, with much love from Grammy. And, as always, to Brian.

Chapter One

She was lost in the wilds of Pennsylvania. Fiona Flanagan peered through her windshield, trying to decipher which of the narrow roads the tilted signpost pointed to. Maybe this wasn't really the wilds, but the only living creature she'd encountered in the last fifteen minutes was the brown-and-white cow that stared mournfully at her from its pasture next to the road.

Clearly the cow wasn't going to help. She frowned down at the map drawn by one of her numerous Flanagan cousins, and decided that squiggly line probably meant she should turn right.

She could always phone her cousin Gabe, but she shrank from having to admit she couldn't follow a few simple directions. Both he and his wife had volunteered to drive her or to get one of his siblings to drive her, but she'd insisted she could do this herself.

The truth was that she'd spent the past two weeks

feeling overwhelmed by the open friendliness offered by these relatives she'd never met before. She'd spent so many years feeling like an outsider in her father's house that she didn't know how to take this quick acceptance.

The pastures on either side of the road gave way to fields of cornstalks, yellow and brown in October. Maybe that was a sign that she was approaching civilization. Or not. She could find her way around her native San Francisco blindfolded, but the Pennsylvania countryside was another story.

The road rounded a bend and there, quite suddenly, was a cluster of houses and buildings that had to be the elusive hamlet she'd been seeking. Crossroads, the village was called, and it literally was a crossroads, a collection of dwellings grown up around the point at which two of the narrow blacktop roads crossed.

Relieved, she slowed the car, searching for something that might be a For Sale sign. The real estate agent with whom she'd begun her search had deserted her when he couldn't interest her in any of the sterile, bland, modern buildings he'd shown her on the outskirts of the busy small city of Suffolk. But she didn't want suburban, she wanted the country. She had a vision of her practice as a nurse-midwife in a small community where she'd find a place to call home.

Through the gathering dusk she could see the glow of house lights in the next block. But most of the village's few businesses were already closed. She drove by a one-pump service station, open, and a minuscule post office, closed. The Penn Dutch Diner had a few lights on, but only five cars graced its parking lot.

The Crossroads General Store, also closed, sat comfortably on her right, boasting a display of harness and tack in one window and an arrangement of what had to be genuine Amish quilts in the other. And there, next to it, was the sign she'd searched for: For Sale.

She drew up in front of the house. It had probably once been a charming Victorian, but now it sagged sadly, as if ashamed of such signs of neglect as cracked windows and peeling paint. But it had a wide, welcoming front porch, with windows on either side of the door, and a second floor that could become a cozy apartment above her practice.

For the first time in days of searching, excitement bubbled along her nerves. This might be it. If she squinted, she could picture the porch bright with autumn flowers in window boxes, a calico cat curled in the seat of a wicker rocker, and a neat brass plate beside the front door: Fiona Flanagan, Nurse-Midwife.

Home. The word echoed in her mind, setting up a sweet resonance. *Home.*

She slid out of the car, taking the penlight from her bag. Tomorrow she could get the key from the reluctant real estate agent, but she'd at least get a glimpse inside in the meantime. She hurried up the three steps to the porch, avoiding a nasty gap in the boards, and approached the window on the left.

The feeble gleam of the penlight combined with the

dirt on the window to thwart her ability to see inside. She rubbed furiously at the glass with a tissue. At a minimum she needed a waiting room, office and exam room, and if—

"What do you think you're doing?" A gruff voice barked out the question, and the beam of a powerful light hit her like a blow, freezing her in place. "Well? Turn around and let me see you."

Heart thudding, she turned slowly, the penlight falling from suddenly nerveless fingers. "I was just l-looking."

Great. She sounded guilty even to herself.

The tall, broad silhouette loomed to enormous proportions with the torchlight in her eyes. She caught a glimpse of some metallic official insignia on the car that was pulled up in front of hers.

The man must have realized that the light was blinding her because he lowered the beam fractionally. "Come down off the porch."

She scrabbled for the wandering penlight, grabbed it and hurried down the steps to the street, trying to pull herself together. Really, she was overreacting. The man couldn't be as big and menacing as she was imagining.

But at ground level with him, she realized that her imagination wasn't really that far off. He must have stood well over six feet, with a solid bulk that suggested he was as immovable as one of the nearby hills. In the dim light, she made out a craggy face that looked as if it had been carved from rock. A badge glinted on his chest.

She rushed to explain. "Really, I didn't mean any

harm. I understand this building is for sale, and I just wanted to have a quick look. I can come back tomorrow with the real estate agent."

She turned toward her car. Somehow, without giving the impression that the mountain had moved, the man managed to be between her and the vehicle.

Her heart began to pound against her ribs. She was alone in a strange place, with a man who was equally strange, and her cell phone was in her handbag, which lay unhelpfully on the front seat of the car she couldn't reach.

"Not so fast," he rumbled. "Let's see some identification, please."

At least she thought he said please—that slow rumble was a little difficult to distinguish. She could make out the insignia on his badge now, and her heart sank.

Crossroads Township Police. Why couldn't she have fallen into the hands of a nice, professional State Trooper, instead of a village cop who probably had an innate suspicion of strangers?

"My driver's license is in my car," she pointed out.

Wordlessly, he stood back for her to pass him and then followed her closely enough to open the door before she could reach the handle. She grabbed her wallet, pulling out the California driver's license and handing it to him.

"Ca-li-for-ni-a." He seemed to pronounce all of the syllables separately.

"Yes, California." Nerves edged her voice. "Is that a problem, Officer?"

She snapped her mouth shut before she could say anything else. Don't make him angry. Never argue with a man who's wearing a large badge on his chest.

"Could be."

She blinked. She almost thought there was a thread of humor in the words.

He handed the ID back. "What brings you to Crossroads Township, Ms. Flanagan?"

"I'm looking for a house to buy. Someone from the real estate office mentioned this place. I got a little lost, or I'd have been here earlier."

She shifted her weight uneasily from one foot to the other as she said the words. That steady stare made her nervous. He couldn't really detain her for looking in a window, could he?

She looked up, considering saying that, and reconsidered at the sight of a pair of intense blue eyes in a stolid face made up entirely of planes. Don't say anything to antagonize him.

"I see." He invested the two words with a world of doubt. "You have anyone locally who can vouch for you?"

Finally she realized what she should have sooner. Of course she had someone to vouch for her. She had a whole raft of cousins. Family. Not a word that usually had much warmth for her, but maybe now—

Ted Rittenhouse saw the relief that flooded the woman's face. She'd obviously come up with a solution she thought would satisfy him.

"I'm staying with a cousin, Gabe Flanagan." She was so relieved that the words tripped over each other. She snatched a cell phone from her bag. "Look, you can call him. He'll vouch for me. Here's my cell phone. You can use it."

"Seems to me I've heard of those newfangled gadgets," he said dryly, pulling his own cell phone from his uniform pocket. "You have his number?"

Even in the dim light provided by the dome lamp of her car, he could see the color that flooded her fair skin at that. He assessed her while he punched in the number she gave him. Slim, erect, with a mane of strawberry-blond hair pulled back from a heart-shaped face.

A pair of intelligent gray eyes met his directly, in spite of the embarrassment that heightened her color. Something about the cut of her tan slacks and corduroy jacket suggested a bit more sophistication than was usually found in Crossroads Township, where the standard attire was jeans, except for the Plain People.

"Mr. Flanagan? This is Ted Rittenhouse, Crossroads Township Police. I've got a young lady here who says she's staying with you. Fiona Flanagan, her name is."

"Fiona? She's my cousin." Quick concern filled the man's voice, wiping away some of Ted Rittenhouse's suspicion. Potential housebreakers didn't usually come equipped with respectable-sounding relatives. "Has she had a car accident? What's wrong?"

"Nothing wrong. She maybe got a little lost is all. I'll guide her back to your place all right." The Pennsylvania Dutch cadence, wiped from his voice during his years in the city, had come back the instant he'd moved back home to Crossroads. "If you'll just give me directions…."

As Flanagan gave him the directions, Ted realized he knew exactly where that farm was. The next township over, but he knew most of the back roads and landmarks in the county, even if that area wasn't his jurisdiction. Somehow you never forget the land that meant home when you were a kid. Maybe that was especially true of a place like this, where the same families had owned farms for generations.

When he slid the phone back in his pocket, he realized Ms. Flanagan was watching him with wariness in those clear eyes.

"It's not necessary for you to guide me anywhere. I can get back to my cousin's on my own."

"No problem at all. It's not out of my way. I'll guide you there."

"I'd prefer to go alone." She enunciated the words as if he was a dumb hick who couldn't understand.

Well, fair enough. In her eyes, he probably was. But he wasn't going to let her just disappear, not until that last faint suspicion was cleared up. As the law in the township, he was responsible and he took it seriously.

"Sorry, ma'am. You heard me tell your cousin I'd guide you home, and I'm not about to let you get lost. Again."

For a moment longer she glared at him, sensing he was poking mild fun at her. Then she jerked a nod, as if to admit defeat, and rounded her car to slide into the driver's seat.

He paused, flashing the light around the old Landers place and then over Ruth Moser's general store next door. Be a good thing if someone bought the Landers place. It had been standing empty too long. But Ruth wouldn't appreciate it if someone up and put a phony Pennsylvania Dutch tourist trap right next to her shop.

Course he didn't know what the Flanagan woman had in mind for the building. He didn't think anyone who dressed like she did would sell plastic Amish dolls made in some third world country.

No sign of life in the general store, and everything looked locked up tight. He'd advised Ruth to put in an alarm system, but so far she hadn't listened. Folks liked to think this was still the quiet countryside it had been fifty years ago, but that wasn't so.

He walked back to the patrol car and slid in. Vandalism, petty crime, the theft of some handmade Amish quilts out at Moses Schmidt's place... Even Crossroads Township had its share of crime. And when he'd pinned this badge on, he'd made a vow to protect and to serve.

A familiar pang went through him at the thought. He pulled out, watching the rearview mirror to be sure the Flanagan woman pulled out behind him. He thought he'd made the right choice in coming back home after the trouble in Chicago, but maybe a man could never know until the end of his life if he'd been following God's leading or his own inclinations.

As it was, there were those he loved who'd never understand his choices. Thank the Lord, they were willing to love him anyway.

At least he'd been coming back to something he knew when he'd come here. What on earth would bring a woman like Fiona Flanagan to buy a place here? The address on her driver's license was San Francisco. Did she have some pie-in-the-sky dream of rural bliss? If so, she'd no doubt be disappointed.

He'd frightened her when he'd accosted her so abruptly, and he was sorry for that. All he'd seen had been a dark figure at the window of the empty house, and he'd reacted automatically. Still, she'd recovered soon enough, ready to flare up at him in an instant.

There was the gate to the Flanagan farm. When he saw the fanciful sign with its cavorting animals, recollection began to come. He'd heard about this place—they trained service animals for the disabled. If she really belonged here, Ms. Flanagan was probably all right.

She tooted her horn, as if to say that he could leave her now. Instead, he turned into the lane and drove up to the house. It was full dark, and it wouldn't hurt to see the woman safely into her cousin's hands.

The farmhouse door opened the moment his lights flashed across the windows, and a man waited outside by the time he came to a stop. The other car drew up under the willow tree with a little spurting of gravel, as if the driver's temper were not quite under control.

He got out, leaving the motor running as he took the hand the man extended. "I'm Ted Rittenhouse."

"Good to meet you. Gabe Flanagan." Flanagan turned to his cousin, who came toward them reluctantly, probably too polite to just walk away from him. "Fiona, we were getting a little worried when you weren't back by dark. I'm glad you ran into someone who could help you get home."

She managed a smile, but he suspected she was gritting her teeth. "Officer Rittenhouse was very helpful."

"It was my pleasure, ma'am." He would have tipped his hat, but he'd left it in the car. "I hope you'll stop by and see me if you ever come to Crossroads again. I'd be glad to be of help to you."

"I'm sure that won't be necessary. Thank you for leading me back." She hesitated a moment, and then she held out her hand.

Surprised, he took it. It felt small but strong in his. "Good night, Ms. Flanagan."

"Good night." She might have wanted to add "good riddance," but either manners or common sense kept a slight smile on her face. She turned and walked toward the house, her back very straight.

Fiona crossed the guest bedroom at Gabe and Nolie's farmhouse a few days later, charmed again by the curve of the sleigh bed and the colorful patchwork quilt. Maybe she'd have something like that in her new house. Her house, officially, as of ten o'clock this morning.

She had to admit she'd hesitated about buying the place in Crossroads after her experience there the other night. But the house was irresistible, and, in the clear light of day, she had to admit the police officer was just doing his duty.

Besides, the lure of the place overrode everything else. *Home,* it kept saying to her. *Home.*

Crossroads, she'd learned, was a fairly large area, encompassing several small villages on the outskirts of Suffolk, as well as farmland. Surely a township police officer like Ted Rittenhouse would be too busy with his other duties to bother about her. Or to annoy her.

She picked up her jacket and slipped it on. October had abruptly turned chilly, at least for the day. Still, anyone who'd grown up in San Francisco was used to changeable weather. That wouldn't bother her.

She paused at the dresser, letting her fingers slip across the painted surface of the rectangular wooden box she'd brought with her across the country. It was all she had of the mother she'd never known. How much had that influenced her decision to come here? She wasn't sure, and she didn't like not being sure about something so important. When her advisor in the nurse-midwife program had mentioned that his part of Pennsylvania had a growing need for midwives, something had lit up inside her. Some instinct had said that here she'd find what she was looking for, even if she didn't quite know what it was.

"That's a replica of a dower chest," Nolie spoke from the doorway. "It's lovely. Did you buy it here?"

Fiona smiled at her hostess. With her fresh-scrubbed face, blond hair pulled back in a ponytail, jeans and flannel shirt, Nolie Flanagan looked more like a teenager than a busy wife and mother, as well as an accomplished trainer of service animals for the disabled.

"I brought it with me. It was my mother's." She hoped the shadow she felt when she said the words didn't show in her voice. "I hate to show my ignorance, but what is a dower chest?"

Nolie came closer, tracing the stiff, painted tulips with their green leaves, fat little hearts and yellow stars in circles that decorated the box. "A traditional dower chest is much larger than this—like a cedar chest—for Pennsylvania Dutch girls to store the linens they make in preparation for their wedding. This smaller one was probably for a child to keep her treasures in."

It hadn't occurred to her that Nolie would be a source of information, but her Aunt Siobhan had said that Nolie's family had lived on this farm for generations. "When you say Pennsylvania Dutch, do you mean Amish?"

Nolie leaned against the dresser, apparently willing to be distracted from whatever chores called her. "The Amish are Pennsylvania Dutch, but not all Pennsylvania Dutch are Amish." She grinned. "Confusing, I know. And to add to the confusion, we aren't really Dutch at all. We're of German descent. William Penn welcomed the early German immigrants, including the Amish. They've held on to their identity better than most because of their religious beliefs."

"It can't be easy, trying to resist the pressures of the modern world."

"No. There are always those who leave the community, like your mother."

Fiona blinked. "I didn't realize you knew about her."

Distress showed in Nolie's blue eyes. "I'm sorry—I didn't pry, honestly. Siobhan mentioned it, when she told us you were coming."

Her Aunt Siobhan and Uncle Joe knew about her mother, probably more than she did, of course. During the week she'd spent in their house she'd wondered if they'd talk about her mother, or about the reason her father hadn't spoken to his brother in over twenty-five years. But they hadn't, and Fiona was too accustomed to not rocking the boat to mention it herself. In any case, the breach between brothers meant they'd know little of what happened after her parents left.

"It's all right. I don't know much about her myself. She died shortly after I was born."

"I'm sorry," Nolie said again. "But your father must have spoken of her."

"No." She transferred her gaze to the chest, because that was easier than looking into Nolie's candid eyes. "My father couldn't take care of me—I was in foster care for years. By the time I went to live with him, he'd remarried."

And he hadn't particularly wanted reminders of that early mistake. She wouldn't say that. She wasn't looking for pity, and she'd already said more than she'd intended.

Nolie's hand closed over hers, startling her, and she repressed the urge to pull away. "I know what that's like. I was in foster care, too. And with a great-aunt who didn't want me. It can be tough to get past that sometimes."

Fiona's throat tightened in response, but the habit of denial was too ingrained. She used the movement of picking up her handbag to draw away.

"It was a long time ago. I don't think much about it now." At least, she tried not to.

Nolie made some noncommittal sound that might have been doubt or agreement, but she didn't push. "I suppose you'll want to look up your mother's family, too, now that you're here."

Fiona shook her head. She'd been over this and over it, and she was sure she'd made the right decision. "I don't plan to do that. It's not the same thing as coming to see the Flanagan family. Aunt Siobhan always tried to keep in touch, and I knew she'd be glad to see me."

"But they probably—"

"No." That sounded too curt. She'd have to explain, at least a little. "My mother's family never made any effort to contact me. The one time my father spoke to me about it, he said they'd rejected my mother for marrying him. It's hardly likely they'd want to see me."

"You can't be sure of that." Nolie's face was troubled. "I'd be glad to help you find them. Or maybe that police officer you met could help."

"No. Thanks anyway." She forced a smile. "I appreciate it, but I've made my decision. I don't want to find them."

Because they rejected your mother? The small voice in the back of her mind was persistent. Or because you're afraid they might reject you?

"If that's what you want—" Nolie began, but her words were interrupted by a wail from downstairs. "Uh-oh." She smiled. "Sounds like trouble. That music video keeps her happy for a half hour, but then only Mommy will do. All my years of taking care of animals didn't prepare me for the demands of one small human."

"And you love it." Fiona picked up her corduroy jacket and handbag. "Go ahead, take care of little Siobhan. I'm fine, really."

Nolie nodded. "If you ever want to talk—"

"Thanks. I'm okay."

The wails soared in pitch, and Nolie spun and trotted down the steps. "Mommy's coming. It's all right."

Fiona followed more slowly. The maternal love in Nolie's face was practically incandescent. Seeing that when it happened for the first time was one of the best rewards of being a midwife. Once her practice got on its feet, she'd have that opportunity again and again.

She was off to take possession of her new house, the first step toward her new life.

Lord, please bless this new beginning. Help me not to dwell on the difficulties of the past, but only on the promises of the future.

Chapter Two

When no one answered his knock at the old Landers house, Ted pulled open the screen door and stepped into the hallway, glancing around. Come to think of it, he'd have to start calling this the Flanagan place. Or Flanagan clinic, maybe. Rumor had it she was starting a midwife practice here.

Whatever she was doing, Ms. Flanagan really shouldn't leave her door standing open that way. Then he noticed that the latch had come loose when he pulled on the screen door, probably one of hundreds of little things to be fixed.

"Ms. Flanagan?"

The two large rooms on either side of the central hallway were empty, except for a few odds and ends of furniture left by the last inhabitants. He could see what attracted the woman to the house—under the dust and neglect were beautiful hardwood floors, and the rooms were graciously proportioned, with bay windows looking out toward the street.

"Hello, is anyone here?"

A muffled call answered him from somewhere upstairs. Taking that for an invitation, he started up the staircase, running his hand along the curving banister. An oval stained-glass window on the landing sent a pattern of color onto the faded linoleum someone had been foolish enough to put over those beautiful stairs.

Sunlight poured through the tall window at one end of the center of the second floor landing. He paused, blinking at the sight of a rickety stepladder under what had to be the opening to the attic. A pair of sneakered feet balanced on the very top. Nothing else was visible of Fiona but a pair of trim legs in dust-streaked jeans.

The stepladder wobbled dangerously, and he grabbed it, steadying it with both hands. "What on earth are you doing up there? Trying to break a leg?"

As soon as the words were out, he realized that was more or less what he'd said that first night when he'd spotted her. Now, at least, she owned the house, but that was no excuse for endangering herself.

Fiona poked her head down from the dark rectangle of the attic opening, looking disheveled and annoyed. "What are you doing here?"

"At the moment, I'm keeping this ladder from collapsing under you."

"It's perfectly fine." Her weight shifted, and the ladder swayed.

He raised an eyebrow. "You want me to let go?"

Her lips clamped together. "No." She seemed to force the word out. Then, hands braced on the edge of the opening, she started lowering herself.

He caught her elbows and lifted her the rest of the way to the floor. The stepladder, relieved, collapsed in a heap on the dusty floorboards.

For a moment Fiona looked as if she'd like to kick the recalcitrant ladder, but then she managed a rueful smile. "Much as I hate to admit it, it looks as if you're right."

"I'll find something sturdy to stand on and close that for you. No problem."

"I'd say I don't need help, but that would just convince you I'm totally irrational." The smile warmed a bit, and her eyebrows lifted. "Did you come for something in particular?"

"Just being neighborly," he said mildly. He glanced around, spotting a solid-looking chair in the nearest room, and hauled it over. Fiona wouldn't be able to reach the ceiling from it, but he could.

He climbed onto the chair, reached up and eased the hatch back into place. It set off a puff of dust as it settled into its groove. He stepped back to the floor.

Fiona, apparently aware of how dirty she was, attempted to transfer the dust from her hands to her jeans, not looking at him. "Thank you."

"Any time."

That fierce independence of hers amused him, but it also made him wonder what was behind it. If she couldn't accept a little nosy neighborliness, she'd never fit in here. He'd had to get used to that again when he came back.

She straightened. "I'm glad this isn't an official call. As you can see, I'm rather busy just now."

"Looking over your new purchase from top to bottom," he agreed. The girls he'd grown up with had had plenty of spirit, giving as good as they got, but Fiona was different. Defensive, almost, and the cop part of his mind wondered what she had to be defensive about.

"It's a beautiful house, really. It's just been neglected." Her smile flickered, and he thought her pride of ownership was getting the better of her wariness with him. "Once I have the renovations done, you won't know it's the same place."

"What do you have in mind to do?" He was happy to keep her talking about the house, because it seemed to put her at ease. Since she was moving in, she was part of his responsibility, and he liked to stay on friendly terms with folks.

"My living quarters will be up here." She gestured. "At first I thought I'd have to install a kitchen on this floor, but there's actually a back staircase that leads down to the current kitchen, so I can just use that."

"A remnant from the days when people had servants, I guess. What happens downstairs?"

"The old parlor will make a perfect waiting room." She started down the steps, gesturing as she talked, and he followed. "The other rooms will have to be partitioned to make an exam room and an office, maybe space for classes. The birthing clinic where I worked in San Francisco ran a lot of childbirth classes, but I don't know how much demand there will be here."

He shrugged, coming down the last step to stand beside her in the hall. "You may be surprised. Plenty of women among the Plain People prefer home births and might enjoy the classes. You should be able to build a good practice, if you stay."

"If?" Her eyebrows shot up at his words. "I'm not going to all this trouble with the intent of leaving. Why would you say that?"

He shrugged. "You wouldn't wonder if you knew how this state has been losing medical personnel to other places. We've seen too much coming and going, mostly going, to take anything for granted. Folks just start to rely on someone and then find they've moved on to greener pastures."

Especially city-bred people like you, he thought but didn't say.

"I'm not going anywhere." She stroked the intricate carving of the newel post. "This place is going to be my home."

Her voice actually trembled with emotion on the last word, touching him, making him want to know what lay behind that emotion, but he didn't figure he had the right.

He was here because it was his duty to protect and serve all the residents of his township, he reminded himself. Not because he had a personal interest in a woman like Fiona Flanagan, with her quick tongue and urban manners.

"Well, if that's what you plan to do with the house, I guess you're going to need someone to do the carpentry work, won't you?"

She nodded. "Is there any chance you might be able to recommend someone?"

"There are a couple of possibilities among the Amish carpenters, it being fall and the harvest is in. I'll see what I can do."

"Amish," she repeated, and he couldn't tell what emotion tightened her face for an instant.

"They're good carpenters, and this is an Amish community. I'd think you'd want an introduction to them."

"Yes, of course, that would be perfect." Whatever the emotion had been, it was gone. "Do you think they'd be able to start soon?"

She looked up at him with such appeal that for a moment he'd do most anything to keep that hope shining in her eyes.

"I'll see if I can get hold of Mose Stetler. Maybe he can come over today or tomorrow."

"Thank you so much." All her wariness was washed away by enthusiasm. "Thank you."

"No problem." He took a reluctant step toward the door. "I'll see what I can do."

And while he was at it, he'd best give himself a good talking to. Fiona's blend of urban sophistication and innocent enthusiasm was a heady mixture, but he couldn't afford to be intrigued by a woman like her. If he ever decided to risk himself on love again, it would be with a nice, ordinary woman who understood the balancing act between two worlds that he maintained every day of his life.

By midafternoon, Fiona had finished cleaning the room intended for her bedroom and even hung some clothes in the closet. It wasn't going to take much more than elbow grease and a little furniture to make her upstairs apartment livable. Now, if Ted came through on his promise to contact the carpenters, she could actually have an opening day in sight.

She'd already gone through the arduous process necessary to get her certification in order, and she'd contacted several obstetricians and the hospital in Suffolk, as well as a birthing center in the city that could use her services on a part-time basis until she got her practice on its feet. Now all that remained was to complete the office and find some clients.

Nolie, who knew the area well, had advised her to build word of mouth by meeting as many people as possible, and she might as well start on that today. After a shower and a change of clothes, she went outside, hesitating for a moment on the porch. She'd much rather be judged on her professional expertise than her personality, but if she planned to build her own practice, this had to be done.

Taking a deep breath and straightening her jacket, she

headed for the general store. She'd already noticed how busy it was, and since it was right next door, it was a logical place to start.

The sign on the front door read Ruth Moser, Proprietor. Maybe Ruth would be the friendly type of neighbor who'd let her post her business card where people would see it. Another deep breath was necessary, and then she opened the door and stepped inside.

The store was bigger than she'd thought from the outside—extending back into almost cavernous depths where aisles were stocked with what she supposed were farming supplies, as well as hardware and tools she couldn't begin to identify. The front part of the store carried groceries, and through an archway she glimpsed what must have been the tourist section—quilts, rag rugs, cloth dolls with blank faces—all the souvenirs a visitor to Pennsylvania Dutch country might want to take home.

"Welcome." The woman who came toward her wore a print dress with an apron over it. A white prayer cap was perched on abundant gray hair pulled back into a bun. Her smile echoed the welcome. "I'll spare you the usual Penn Dutch spiel. You're not a tourist." She held out her hand. "I'm Ruth Moser."

Fiona found her hand caught in a grip as strong as a man's. "I'm Fiona Flanagan. I just bought the house next door."

"And you're a nurse-midwife," Ruth finished for her. "We already know that about you, we do. Hard to keep any secrets in a place like Crossroads, believe me."

The woman's smile was contagious. Bright blue eyes in a weathered face inspected Fiona, but it was a friendly inspection that she didn't find intimidating.

"I guess I don't need the explanation I'd planned to give you then, do I?"

"Ach, well, you'll have to forgive us. Folks who live in an area like this all know each other so well that an incomer is a nine days' wonder. Everyone in the township knows about the new midwife, and welcome news it is. The closest Amish midwife is nearly twenty miles away, and folks out here don't like going clear into Suffolk, either."

"I'm certainly glad to hear that." This was going better than she'd imagined. "I'd hoped you might be willing to post one of my business cards where your customers would see it."

"Give me a whole stack of them, and I'll pass them on to anyone who might be thinking of babies," Ruth said promptly.

"That's wonderful." She pulled a handful from the side pocket of her bag. "I'll bring some more over later, if you can use them."

"Sure thing." Ruth took the cards and slipped them into an apron pocket. "I suppose Ted Rittenhouse told you how short of medical help we are around here, unless we want to go into Suffolk."

Why would she suppose anything of the kind? "Ted Rittenhouse?"

Ruth seemed oblivious to the edge in her voice. "Ted

certainly is a nice fellow. Born and bred in the township, and glad we were to have him come back home again after that time in Chicago. You like him, don't you?"

"I—I thought he was very helpful. When I got lost, I mean, the first time I came to see the house."

"Helpful, yes. Kind, too. Why, I've known that boy since he was running around barefoot. There's not a mean bone in his body."

"Yes, well—I'm sure that's true." And why on earth did the woman think she needed to know that? "Do you mind if I look around your store?"

"I'll show you around myself. Not exactly busy on a weekday in the fall, though weekends we still get the rush of tourists trampling through, oohing and aahing over the Amish and blocking the roads every time they spot a buggy. Still, their money helps keep me afloat."

"You seem to carry just about everything anyone could want in here." A cooler marked Night Crawlers sat next to a rack filled with the latest celebrity magazines.

"That's why it's a general store." Ruth looked around with satisfaction at her domain. Apparently she felt the same way about her store as Fiona did about her practice. "I have something for everyone from the Amish farmers to the senior citizen bus tours. No good Pennsylvania Dutchman ever turned down profit."

Fiona glanced at the woman's print dress. "You're not Amish, I take it?"

"Mennonite. First cousins to the Amish, you bet."

She brushed the full skirt. "You can tell by the clothes. You'll soon get onto it." The bell on the door tinkled, and she gestured toward the archway. "I'll just get that. Go on through and check out the other section. I've got some lovely quilts and handmade chests if you're looking to furnish your house local."

She hadn't thought of that, but obviously it would be good public relations to buy some of what she needed locally. She walked through the archway. The rag rugs would be beautiful against the hardwood once the floors were cleaned and polished. And—

She rounded the end of the aisle and lost her train of thought. The back part of this area was a large, well-lit workroom. Finished quilts lined the walls, their colors and patterns striking.

Two Amish women bent over a quilt frame, apparently putting the finishing touches to a quilt whose vibrant colors glowed against their dark, plain dresses. Another sat at a treadle sewing machine. All three glanced at her briefly and then lowered their eyes, as if it were impolite to stare.

But she was the one who was being impolite, unable to tear her gaze away. Was that what her mother would have looked like now, if she hadn't run away, if she hadn't died? Dark dress, dark apron, hair parted in the center and pulled back beneath a white cap, seeming to belong in another century?

"Looks like plenty of work is being done in here." The voice from behind startled her into an involuntary movement. Ted nodded coolly and strolled past her to lean over the quilt on the frame.

"Another Double Wedding Ring? Haven't you made enough of those in the last year, Em?"

The woman he spoke to surprised Fiona by laughing up at him in what could only be described as a flirtatious way. "That's what the English want, Ted Rittenhouse. You know that well, you do."

"Well, give the customers what they want, I suppose." He nodded toward Fiona, apparently not noticing that she stood frozen to the spot. "You meet the new midwife who's setting up next door, did you?"

Apparently now that he had, in effect, introduced her, it was all right to stare. Three pairs of eyes fixed on her as Ted mentioned the women's names: Emma Brandt, Barbara Stoller, Sarah Bauman. Emma was probably in her thirties, although it was difficult to judge, and the other two probably in their sixties.

Fiona nodded, trying to get past the unexpected shock she'd felt at the sight of them. These were people who might introduce her to prospective clients in the Amish community, so she'd better try to make a decent impression.

"It's a pleasure to meet you. The quilt is wonderful. I didn't realize you actually made them here."

"Ruth says the tourists like to see the work done." Emma seemed to be the spokeswoman for the group. "We do special orders for folks, too."

"That's great." Fiona knew how stupid she sounded,

but she couldn't seem to help herself. She'd assumed all Amish women were cloistered at home, taking care of their families, instead of out earning money. How much more didn't she know about her mother's people?

Ted strolled back toward her. "Could I have a moment of your time? I'll walk out with you."

She nodded, saying goodbye to the quilters, and preceded him toward the exit. When the door closed, its bell tinkling, he spoke before she could get a word out.

"I'd say if you want to have an Amish clientele for that practice of yours, you'll have to stop looking at them like they're animals in the zoo."

"I didn't!" But she probably had. "I was just surprised, that's all. I didn't realize anyone was back there." How did the man always manage to put her in the wrong?

"Uh-huh." He managed to infuse the syllables with such doubt that her embarrassment was swallowed up in anger. She certainly wasn't going to tell him what had precipitated her behavior.

"Excuse me. I have things to do." She turned, but he stopped her with a hand on her arm.

"Don't you even want to know what I had to tell you?"

She gritted her teeth. Be polite, Fiona. "Of course. What is it?"

"The carpenters will be coming around in an hour or so. Try to get over your feelings about the Amish before then, will you?"

Before she could respond, he walked off across the street.

* * *

"Well, it's not exactly what I expected." Fiona cradled the cell phone against her ear with one hand and continued scrubbing the kitchen sink with the other. She might have to rub all the enamel off to get it clean.

"Better or worse?" Tracy Wilton, her closest friend from midwife training, sounded as if she were in the next room instead of three thousand miles away. "You could always come back, you know. They haven't filled your job here yet."

"I'm not sure whether it's better or worse, but it's definitely different." She thought of Ted's obvious doubt that she'd stick it out. "I'm staying, though. I'll make it work."

"I bet you will. Listen, if your practice gets too big for one person, just give me a call. Especially if you've found any great-looking men among those Pennsylvania Dutch farmers of yours."

Fiona pushed an image of Ted Rittenhouse from her mind. "I'm not looking for any. Trust me. Getting my practice up and running is enough to occupy me for the moment. All I'm worried about right now is whether my money will hold out that long."

A rap sounded on the front door, and she headed into the hallway. "Listen, Tracy, someone's here. I'll give you a call later, okay?"

"Okay. Take care."

Fiona snapped off the phone as she swung the door open and saw what appeared to be a whole congregation of Amish men in black trousers and dark shirts filling her porch. She blinked against the late-afternoon sunlight and realized there were only four, surveying her silently.

What on earth?—and then she realized they had to be the carpenters Ted had said he'd send. The oldest man, his beard a snowy white, nodded gravely.

"I am Mose Stetler. Ted Rittenhouse said as how you are wanting some carpentry work done. Said you needed it in a hurry."

"Yes, he told me he'd talked to you. I'm Fiona Flanagan." She nodded to the men and held the door wide. "Please, come in. I'm glad you were able to come so soon."

And a little surprised Ted hadn't told them to forget about coming after their exchange earlier.

"Oh, we had to." He jerked his head toward the youngest of the men, hardly more than a boy, with rounded cheeks above a rather straggly beard. "Young Aaron, here, he'll be needing your services before long, won't you, Aaron?"

The boy blushed, his prominent ears reddening. "My Susie…" He stopped, apparently embarrassed to actually say that his wife was expecting.

"Well, then, all the more reason to get my practice up and running. But I'll be happy to talk to your wife anytime, even if my office isn't ready." She started to say the woman could phone her, and then realized that she couldn't. "Just have her send a message if she'd like to talk."

He bobbed his head, flushing when one of the other men said something to him in what sounded like

German. She didn't understand the words, but the teasing was obvious.

"So, now." Mr. Stetler rubbed callused palms together. "You show me what you want done, and I will figure out a price." His eyes twinkled. "A fair price. You're one of us, after all."

She blinked. Surely he couldn't be referring to her mother. No one knew except the Flanagans. "One of you?"

"A resident, not a tourist," he explained. Apparently tourists were fair game, but not someone who planned to live here.

She showed them over the downstairs, explaining what she needed. Mose made several helpful suggestions for the arrangement that she hadn't thought of.

Finally he took out a stub of pencil and a scrap of paper and figured a price. She looked at the paper with a sense of relief. It was high, but she'd known it would be, with the cost of materials, and it was well within her budget.

"Fine. We have a deal. When can you start?"

Stetler beamed. "Right away. We do some measurements now, and then be back here at eight o'clock tomorrow morning."

"Excellent."

By the time they'd finished up the measurements and were heading out the door, they were on a first-name basis, even with Aaron, the shy expectant father. She was just assuring him that he wasn't going to feel a thing when one of the other men said something that made them all double over with laughter.

"He said unless Aaron's wife hits him for getting her into that predicament."

Somehow she wasn't surprised to see Ted Rittenhouse standing by the porch, one large boot propped against the front step and a grin on his face.

"I'll protect him," Fiona shot back, her gaze challenging his. She'd let him see that she was getting along perfectly well with his Amish friends.

Ted nudged at the step with his boot. "Hey, Mose, you'd best put fixing this step at the top of your list."

Mose nodded gravely. "Before you put your big foot through it, yes." For some reason, everyone thought that was funny, and they all trooped off, laughing, toward the wagon and its patiently waiting horse.

She was very aware of Ted, standing silent beside her. When he didn't speak, she realized there was something she had to say. She turned toward him, and found him watching her.

"Thank you very much for sending Mose and his crew over. I'm so relieved to have the project underway."

"They'll do a good job for you. And they'll be honest about the price, too."

She nodded. "I'm sure they will." She hesitated, and then decided she'd better say the rest of what she'd been thinking. "You know, I thought maybe you'd change your mind and tell them not to come."

He looked surprised. "Why would I do that?"

"Well, you weren't exactly happy with me earlier."

"That doesn't mean I'd make things difficult for

you. Maybe you have something to learn about folks around here."

Those words might have been said snidely, but she couldn't detect anything other than genuine concern in his voice. Concern, and perhaps even kindness.

"Maybe so." She struggled to speak over the sudden lump in her throat. "This move is a big change in my life. I know I have to adjust some of my attitudes if I'm going to make a go of it here."

His lips twitched in a slight smile. "You'll be fine. You have something to offer. Just give yourself a chance. And give us one, too."

The gentleness in his voice drew her. She looked up to find his intense gaze so focused on her face that it seemed to generate warmth. She couldn't look away, couldn't even seem to draw breath. Was it the afternoon sunlight dazzling her eyes, or was it the man?

And then he took a step back. It was hard to tell with that stolid face of his, but she had a feeling he felt just as shocked as she did.

Chapter Three

Her mother's box now sat on her brand-new dresser in her own bedroom in the house in Crossroads. Fiona touched it, smiling a little at the sound of hammering from downstairs.

She'd moved in yesterday, in spite of Nolie and Gabe's repeated urging to stay with them until the work was completely finished. Much as she'd appreciated their kindness, she'd given in to the need to be here, on the spot, supervising the renovations.

She had a bedroom and a kitchen—at the moment she didn't need anything else. Once she'd found time to paint the room that was going to be her living room, to say nothing of getting some furniture in it, she'd be ready to entertain. She could invite her Flanagan cousins over.

The past few days had been busy ones, notable only for the absence of one person. Ted hadn't dropped by again. Maybe he was occupied with township business.

Or maybe he'd been as shocked by that moment of rapport as she had been.

In any event, it was fine that he hadn't been around. She'd been able to write the incident off as nothing— just a random flare of attraction that she could quickly forget. She had nothing in common with a man like Ted Rittenhouse, and even if she'd wanted it, she had no time in her life for romance.

Making a success of her practice had to be the only thing on her mind now, and she'd already made a good start. An invitation had been relayed by Aaron from his wife and had resulted in her first visit to an Amish home.

The simple, painted interior with its large, square rooms and handmade furniture had charmed her. When she'd commented on the beauty of a hand-carved wooden rocking chair, young Susie had shrugged off the compliment, saying the chair was "for use, not for pretty."

She'd been surprised to find Susie already in her thirty-fourth week, but she learned that the couple had only recently returned to the family farm after living in an Amish community in Ohio where Aaron was apprenticed to a master carpenter. Susie was healthy, happy and eagerly looking forward to the birth, and especially to having her baby at home. Fiona had come away with a sense of satisfaction that she would provide the kind of birthing experience the couple wanted.

And happy that she was wanted and needed—she couldn't deny that. It was a step toward belonging. And another step might be—

She lifted the lid on the box, her fingers touching the perfectly matched corners. Here was all she had of the mother she'd never known. An Amish cap and apron, put away never to be worn again. A white baby gown, edged with delicate embroidery. And the patches for a quilt, each one sewn with stitches so tiny they were practically invisible.

She carried the pieces to the spool bed which was her latest purchase and spread them out, not sure how they were intended to fit together. Each piece was a rectangle composed of smaller square and rectangular pieces in rich, solid colors. The deep pink shade that predominated made her wonder if her mother might have intended the quilt for a daughter. If so, she'd never know.

But she could have the quilt. She didn't have the skill to put it together, but the quilters at Ruth's store did. She could imagine it gracing her bed, symbolizing her ties to her new community.

She gathered the pieces, slipped them into a bag and went quickly down the steps, greeting the carpenters, amazed as always by how much they'd accomplished. The rooms were taking shape before her eyes, and her dream was closer to reality every day.

She hurried over to the general store, eager now to set this project in motion. Ruth looked up when the bell tinkled, but she was busy with a customer, so Fiona waved and went on through to the workroom. Emma Brandt greeted her with a smile, while two older women she hadn't seen before glanced up, nodded and bent over the quilt frame again.

"Emma, I'd like to show you something." She approached the quilt frame slowly. It wasn't too late to change her mind, but Emma was nodding. Waiting.

"Yes?"

For a moment her hand held the bag shut. This would be the first time she'd shown the quilt squares to anyone, and she felt an odd reluctance to have them out of her possession. Shaking the emotion off, she drew out the fabric squares.

"I have these quilt pieces, and I wondered if you'd be able to put them together for me."

Emma pushed her glasses into place and took them, turning them slowly in her capable hands. "A log cabin design," she said. "The colors are lovely. This will make a fine quilt for your new bed."

She was getting used to the fact that everyone seemed to know everything about her. It seemed the rumor mill was always grinding in Crossroads. Emma could probably tell her where she'd bought the bed and how much she'd paid for it.

"That's what I thought, although I don't even know how the squares fit together." She may as well admit her ignorance up front.

Emma quickly moved some of the blocks together. "The traditional manner would be to arrange them like this, so that the darker colors make diagonal lines across the surface."

The quilt seemed to come to life under her hands, and Fiona could visualize it on her bed. Maybe she could find curtains in one of the solid colors.

"That would be perfect. Do you have time to finish it for me?"

"I'm sure we can." Emma picked up one of the pieces, examining it closely. "The workmanship is very fine, uh-huh. Did you make it yourself?"

Fiona shook her head. "It's all I can do to sew a button on. These were given to me. I was told that my mother made them."

"Ah." Emma's look of sympathy said she understood. "Then very special the quilt will be for you."

"Yes." She willed away the lump in her throat. "It will be very special."

One of the older women rose from the quilting frame. She walked toward them, her faded blue eyes magnified by the thick glasses she wore. She reached for the quilt pieces, turning them over in work-worn hands.

Emma said something in the low German that Fiona had learned was the common tongue of the Amish. For a moment the older woman stood frozen. Then she said something that made Emma give an audible gasp.

Their expressions startled Fiona. "Emma, is something wrong?"

Emma shook her head, not looking up. Then, so quickly Fiona hardly understood what was happening, all three women folded up their work and scurried away without a word.

* * *

By evening, Fiona was feeling thoroughly exasperated with all things Amish. Ruth had had no explanation for what happened and seemed as mystified by the women's behavior as Fiona. She'd promised to talk to Emma and try to smooth things over as soon as she could.

But that hadn't been the worst of it. The carpenters had left for lunch as usual, but they hadn't come back. They hadn't sent word, either. They were just gone, with tools left lying where they'd put them down.

Clearly she'd offended someone, but how, she didn't know. She'd have been happy to apologize for whatever it was, but since she couldn't get in touch with any of them that was impossible.

She walked slowly from one unfinished room to another. What if they didn't come back? Panic touched her. Would she be able to find someone else to finish the work? She pulled her cardigan tighter around her. She'd had her share of feeling isolated and helpless in her life, and she didn't like the sensation.

A knock on the door came as a relief. At last, maybe someone was coming to explain. She yanked the door open to find Ted on her porch, frowning down at her.

"We have to talk," he said.

She nodded, stood back for him to enter, and gestured down the hall. "Come back to the kitchen. It's the only finished room downstairs."

She followed him down the hallway, his tall frame blocking out the dim light she had left on in the office.

Reaching the kitchen, she switched the light on and the room sprang to life.

Originally it had been one of those huge, inconvenient rooms that had probably given the cook fallen arches, but at some point it had been renovated. Now the stove, sink and refrigerator made a convenient work triangle, and her few dishes were arranged in the closest of the glass-fronted cabinets.

She started to offer Ted a seat, but he'd already planted large fists on the round pine table. And he didn't look as if he planned to sit down and relax any time soon. He wore jeans and a blue sweater that made his eyes even bluer, but from the way he leaned toward her, he didn't seem any less intimidating than when he wore the uniform.

He didn't need to glare at her as if she'd committed a cardinal sin. A little flare of anger warmed her.

"You may as well stop looking at me that way. I've obviously made a mistake and offended someone, but I don't have the slightest idea what I've done." She folded her arms.

Ted's face was at its most wooden. "Why didn't you tell me you were Hannah Stolzfus's daughter?"

For a moment she could only stare at him. How could he— "How do you know that? I didn't tell anyone here."

"It's true, then? You're actually her child?" The passion in his voice reverberated through the room.

She hugged herself tighter as if to shield herself from him. "Not that it's any of your business, but yes, my mother's name was Hannah Stolzfus. She died shortly after I was born, so I never knew her, but I've seen the birth certificate. That was her name."

His jaw seemed to harden, if that was possible. "Why did you come here?"

She looked at him blankly. "You already know why I came here. To open my practice. What on earth is going on? Why did those women walk out of Ruth's today after they saw my quilt pieces? Why did the carpenters leave?"

"You really don't understand, do you?" Frustration edged his tone.

"Understand what?" She had plenty of her own frustration to go around. "Why is everyone talking in riddles?"

"All right. No riddles." His hands pressed against the table so hard it might collapse under his weight. "Just straightforward English words. Emma Brandt is the younger sister of Hannah Stolzfus. And the older woman who looked at those quilt pieces and recognized them is her mother, Louise Stolzfus."

Her mother, Louise Stolzfus. My grandmother. She could say the words in her head, but not out loud. She tried to stop the inward shaking that she couldn't let him see.

"I didn't know." She spaced the words out clearly. "Don't you understand? I had no idea anyone would recognize those quilt pieces. No idea that Emma Brandt was any relation to my mother. No idea that my mother's family was even still around here."

Ted obviously wasn't convinced. He straightened, folding his arms. "Do you expect me to believe that?"

"I don't expect anything of you!" She snapped the words and immediately regretted it. Getting angry at Ted wouldn't help matters any.

Please, Lord, help me deal with this—with him—in the right way.

"Look, I'm sorry." She thrust her hand into her hair, shoving it back from her face. "Can't we talk about this sensibly, instead of sniping at each other?"

His eyes were watchful, but he jerked a reluctant nod. "All right. Talk."

She frowned, trying to get her mind around everything he'd said. "Are you sure about this? Emma is surely too young to be my mother's sister. Maybe it's a different family altogether."

Some of the harshness seemed to go out of his face. "I'm sure. Amish families are often spread out over a lot of years. Hannah was the eldest, fifteen years older than Emma, who is the youngest."

"I see." She had to admit he seemed sure of his facts. "Even if what you say is true, I'm not sure what all the fuss is about. I'm sorry for startling them with the quilt, and obviously I'll get someone else to finish it for me."

"And you think that will resolve the problem?" He looked at her as if she were a creature from another planet.

The anger flickered again, but under it was a desolation she wouldn't give in to.

"I don't know what else I can do or say. I didn't come here looking for my mother's family, and I don't particularly want anything to do with them. Maybe we can just chalk it up to an unfortunate coincidence and get on with our lives."

Ted had to remind himself that a city-bred creature like Fiona had no idea what she was talking about when it came to family relationships in a place like Crossroads. He'd pity her, if her coming wasn't creating such a problem for people he cared about, people he had to protect.

"Did you actually think you could come here and not run into your mother's family? Why else would you pick Crossroads Township to settle in, if not to find them?"

She shrugged, hugging her slim frame as if she needed protection from him. Her face was very pale, but her gray eyes blazed with life. With anger, probably aimed at him.

"I came to this area because it had a need for nurse-midwives, that's why. And because I wanted to get to know the Flanagans, my father's relatives. I didn't have any ulterior motives, and I certainly have no desire to intrude on my mother's family."

"Why not?" He shot the question at her. "You admit you came to get to know your father's family. Why not your mother's?"

Her lips tightened into a firm line. She was probably thinking this wasn't his business, but he intended to know the truth if he had to stand here all night.

"Because they rejected her." The words burst out of her. "My mother. They turned away from her because she married an outsider. Why would I want a relationship with them now? They haven't bothered about me all these years."

"That's not how it was." He remembered all he'd heard, all he'd known. "She's the one who left. She deserted them, not the other way around, and they've never recovered from that."

"How do you know so much about it?" Suspicion edged her tone.

Emma had only been three when her sister left, but she'd remembered how her mother had aged overnight, how all the happiness seemed to go out of the house with Hannah. And he remembered how she'd cried in his arms when she'd told him she couldn't do the same thing to her parents that her sister had done.

He stiffened. Some things Fiona didn't have the right to know, especially that.

"It's a small community," he said. "I don't think you realize how small. I've been a friend of the family for a long time. I know how much the Stolzfus family grieved when Hannah left. I don't want to see them hurt again."

"I don't want to hurt them. I don't want to have anything to do with them." She thrust her hands through her reddish-blond mane as if she'd pull it out in her frustration. "Can't you just accept that?"

He watched her steadily, trying to read the truth in those gray eyes. Did she really believe what she was saying?

"No," he said slowly. "I can't accept that. How can I, when all of your actions have brought you to a place where you're bound to run into them? You say it's not intentional, and maybe that's so. But the results are the same, and people I care about are already hurting as a result."

"I'm sorry." She stood very straight, facing him, her face pale and set. "Sorry if this hurts them, and sorry you don't believe me. But they rejected my mother, and—"

"Will you stop saying that?" He took a step toward her, as if his very nearness might convince her to believe him. "They did not turn her away."

Her face was like stone. "I read about the Amish, once I was old enough to understand that's what my mother had been. I read about how they shun people who don't do what they're supposed to."

"That proves the old saying, doesn't it?" He sighed in frustration. Did he have to give the woman a crash course in what it meant to be Amish? "'A little learning is a dangerous thing.' It's true that someone might be separated from the congregation to help him see the error of his ways, but that doesn't apply in this case."

"What do you mean?" Doubt flickered in her face.

"Hannah was seventeen when she left, not yet a baptized member of the church, so she didn't break any vows by what she did. I'm sure her parents didn't approve of her choice, but if she'd stayed, they would have made peace with it. They never had the chance. If she'd come back, anytime, they probably would have welcomed her."

Fiona shook her head stubbornly. "How can you say that? They never attempted to get in touch with her after she left. And after she died, they never tried to find me. My whole life, I've never heard a word from them."

Her pain reached out and grabbed his heart, and for a moment he couldn't speak. The urge to comfort her was so strong he had to fight it back. He could pity her, yes, but his loyalties lay elsewhere.

"Fiona, what makes you think they knew you existed?"

He saw that hit her, saw the doubt and pain in her eyes, and thought he'd be a long time regretting that he'd put it there. But it had to be done. This was a bad situation, and an impulsive act on her part could make it even worse.

He shook his head. "I'm sorry," he said again. "Could be you think I'm interfering, and maybe I am. But the best thing you can do now is to stay away from the family. You don't begin to understand them, and you can't judge them by your California standards. Just leave them alone, before you cause each other more pain than you can bear."

Chapter Four

Twenty-four hours had passed since that difficult confrontation with Ted, and Fiona still hadn't shaken off the feelings it had brought on. She dried the few dishes that sat in the dish drainer, glancing out the kitchen window as she did so.

It was dusk already. Yellow light glowed from the windows of the few houses behind hers, partially obscured by the trees, looking distant and lonely. If she'd been looking for privacy when she came here, she'd certainly found it.

In more ways than one, it seemed. The carpenters hadn't turned up again today, and when she'd gone to the store to speak to Ruth about it, she found that the quilters were missing as well.

Ruth had been sympathetic, but her only advice had been to be patient. Sooner or later, the situation would resolve itself. Until then, there was no point in pressing.

She could admire the older woman's patience, but not emulate it. The need to get on with things drove her to pace across the kitchen and back again.

Lord, I don't know what to do. Was Ted right about me? Did I really come here because I wanted to be accepted by my mother's family? If so, it looks as if Your answer to that is no. Please, guide me now.

She blinked back unaccustomed tears, appalled at herself. There was little point in crying over something that had been over and done with before she was born. She couldn't influence it now.

"And we know that in all things, God works for the good of those who love Him, who have been called according to His purpose."

The verse from Romans had always resonated in her heart, but how did she even know that God had called her here? She'd told herself she was following God's leading for her life when she'd made the decision, but if Ted was right about her, maybe she'd only been following her own unconscious desires.

She hung the dish towel on the wooden rack, aligning it as neatly as if that were the most important thing in the world right now. Well, maybe not important, but at least it was something she could control, unlike everything else that had happened lately.

A noise from the unpaved drive that ran behind the house startled her, sending her pulse beating a little more rapidly. Someone was there, but she didn't expect anyone. She went quickly to the door, pulling aside the lace curtain that screened the glass panel so she could peer out.

If a UFO had landed, she couldn't have been more surprised. An Amish buggy had pulled up next to the back step. The horse dropped its head to nibble at the sparse grass. A slim girl in a black cape slid down, turning to say something to the person who held the reins. In a moment he was down, too, and both of them headed toward the door.

They stepped into the pool of light from the lamp above the door. Young, both of them, probably not more than sixteen. She'd never seen either of them before.

She took a breath. If the Amish community intended to tell her to leave, they certainly wouldn't send two teenagers. She opened the door.

"Hello. I'm Fiona Flanagan. Are you looking for me?"

"Yes, we come to see you." The girl, who apparently was the spokesperson, gave a short nod, her dark bonnet bobbing. She had a pretty, heart-shaped face, a pert, turned-up nose and a pair of lively blue eyes. "I am Rachel Stolzfus. We are cousins."

"Cousins?" For a moment she could only gape at the girl, and then she stepped back, holding the door wide. "Please, come in. I'm sorry, did you say you are my cousin?"

"Cousin, yes." The girl, Rachel, came in and then spun toward her, her black cape swinging out. "This is my friend Jonah Felder."

The boy nodded, flushed to the tips of his ears. He

entered, but stood just inside the door, as if ready to bolt back out in an instant.

"I'm happy to meet both of you." And more than a little puzzled. "Won't you sit down?" She gestured toward the straight-backed kitchen chairs. "I'm afraid the rest of the house isn't ready for visitors."

Rachel shook her head at the offer of seats. "We cannot stay long. We are on our way home from visiting Jonah's parents."

She took off her bonnet, though, revealing corn-silk blond hair parted in the center and pulled back into a knot that was covered by a prayer cap.

"But I had to stop and see my new cousin." Her eyes sparkled. "I wanted to be the first, except for Aunt Emma and my grandmother."

Something tightened inside Fiona at that. Her grandmother hadn't even wanted to look at her, much less speak to her. Still, that wasn't Rachel's fault.

"I'm glad you did, but I wouldn't want you to get into any trouble."

"No one will guess that we stopped here." She darted a glance toward Jonah, as if commanding his silence. Her black cape swung open, revealing the deep rose of the dress she wore beneath.

Fiona's heart clenched. "Your dress is the same shade as the rose in my quilt pieces."

Rachel brushed the full skirt with her hand. "Maybe my aunt Hannah had a dress like this. It's only after joining the church that women wear the dark colors. When a garment has no further use, it is cut up for quilting."

"I see." She did see, in a way. A picture of the mother she'd never known was beginning to form in her mind— a smiling girl whose rose dress brought out the roses in her cheeks. "Tell me, how are we related?"

"My father, Daniel, was younger brother to your mother, Hannah." Rachel beamed. "We are cousins. So you see, it is right for me to call on you."

It sounded as if she were trying to convince herself. "Is that what your parents would say?" The last thing she needed was to cause a fight over encouraging Rachel's teenage rebellion.

Rachel shrugged. "Not exactly. Everyone is waiting for my grandfather to decide how we should act. But I didn't want to wait."

Anger spurted up at Rachel's description of the family's reaction. Rachel's grandfather—her grandfather, too—would decide whether the rest of the family should speak to her. She'd told herself she didn't want anything to do with them, so why did that hurt?

"Rachel, I appreciate your coming to see me, but I don't want to get you into trouble. Maybe you should go."

Jonah shuffled his feet. "Ja, Rachel. It is time we were home."

Rachel tossed her head. "Some things I can decide for myself. Besides, Ted Rittenhouse is your friend, and he is an old friend to my family, too. He and my aunt Emma courted when they were young, they did."

That was a tidbit of information about Ted she'd have to consider later.

"I'm happy you came, but maybe you should get on home. It'll be night soon." The thought of them out on a dark highway in that buggy sent a chill down Fiona's spine. That couldn't be safe. "I hope we'll meet again."

A loud rap on the door put a period to her words. Rachel grabbed Jonah's hand, and both of them looked as if they'd been caught raiding the pantry.

Somehow, even through the curtain, there was no mistaking that tall, broad figure. She gave them a reassuring smile and opened the door. It was Ted, of course.

"I wasn't expecting you." That was an understatement. Ted had a way of showing up at the most inconvenient times.

"No, I guess not." Ted stepped inside, not waiting for an invitation. "And you two weren't expecting me either, I'll bargain."

He frowned at the two teenagers, but instead of looking intimidated, as Fiona anticipated, Rachel gave him a saucy smile. "Not expecting, no. But we are not doing anything wrong, Mr. Policeman."

"Your parents might not agree to that."

Rachel pouted, obviously sure of her relationship with him. "You won't tell. Everyone knows the kinds of things you got up to when you were our age."

Was that actually a twinkle in Ted's steely blue eyes? "I might have to arrest you for blackmailing an officer of the law, Miss Rachel."

"We were on our way out." Jonah tugged at Rachel's sleeve. "I will see Rachel safe home, I will."

Rachel let herself be led to the door. "I will see you again, Cousin Fiona. Soon."

"I'll look forward to it."

She tried to ignore the disapproving look Ted sent her way. This was not any of his business, no matter how much he might think otherwise.

She went to the door to see them off, and Ted followed the teens outside. "You have your lights and reflectors on properly, Jonah?"

The boy nodded, climbing up to the buggy. Fiona watched from the doorway as Ted walked around to the back of the buggy, apparently double-checking the orange reflective triangle and the blinking red warning light that must have worked off some sort of battery when Jonah flipped it on.

"All right, then." He came back around and smacked the horse on its rump. "Get along home, you two."

Fiona heard Rachel giggle as Jonah slapped the reins, and the buggy moved slowly off toward the road. Regret slid through her. Would Rachel come back? It hardly seemed likely if her parents heard about this little visit.

She stepped out onto the back stoop. "You won't tell Rachel's parents about this, will you? She didn't mean any harm."

"No. I won't." He planted one foot on the low step and leaned against the railing. The soft glow from the light over the door caught them in its small circle, picking up glints of gold in Ted's thick brown hair. "And you don't need to tell me this wasn't your idea. I know full well it was Rachel's."

At least he didn't sound angry, with the kids or with her. "I was—well, astonished. I didn't realize Amish kids had that much freedom."

"The rumspringa," he said. "I suppose you don't know about that."

She folded her arms across her chest, drawing her sweater close around her.

"Tell me about it."

"It's a time when Amish teenagers get to taste the outside world, generally when they're between sixteen and twenty. Sowing wild oats, I suppose you might say. A time when they go courting, too."

It flashed through her mind, then, what Rachel had said about Ted courting her aunt. Flashed through, and was quickly dismissed. She didn't know him well enough to ask him about his personal life, even though he didn't hesitate to intrude in hers.

"They seem too young for that."

He shrugged. "They'll probably be married by the time they're in their early twenties. But before they are baptized into the church, they have the chance to explore the world a little. It's a way to make sure the Amish life is really what they want."

"So it wasn't that bad—Rachel coming to see me?"

He frowned. "That's another thing altogether. If her parents forbade her to see you, she shouldn't disobey. And they wouldn't appreciate your encouraging her."

"I didn't. How could I possibly encourage it? I had no idea who she was until she explained the connection. She was just curious about me. Haven't you ever been curious?"

His gaze rested on her for a long moment, and her breath seemed to catch in her throat at the warmth in his eyes.

"Yes, I have been curious." For a moment she almost thought he'd add, *about you.* "But I am not sixteen. Or Amish."

"You just said her parents gave her more freedom now." She rushed the words. It was safer to keep the conversation on Rachel, not on Ted, because otherwise she might read too much into the way he was looking at her.

"That doesn't mean they don't worry about her. About the influence of English people on her."

"English?"

"World people. Those who are not Amish." His expression lightened. "The world calls the Amish Pennsylvania Dutch, when they're really German. So the Amish call all outsiders English."

"People like me." She got it, finally. "You mean they wouldn't want her to be around me because they're afraid of the influence I might have on her." She straightened. "That's so far-fetched it's ridiculous."

"Is it?" He looked at her steadily, and that stolid face of his didn't give anything away. The growing darkness pressed around them, reminding her of that first night, trapped in the beam of his flashlight.

"Yes." The word came out defiantly. She wouldn't let him intimidate her into saying she'd turn Rachel away from her door, if that's what he had in mind.

"You're forgetting." His voice was quiet, but there was suppressed emotion in his intent eyes. "But they haven't. It was during her rumspringa that Hannah met your father. She turned her back on everything that was important to her. They never saw her again."

She took an involuntary step away from him, trying to frame a response through the chaos his words set off in her mind. But Ted turned and disappeared into the darkness.

"And today they all reappeared without a word of explanation." Fiona glanced across the front seat of Nolie's battered old station wagon.

Nolie lifted her hands from the wheel for a second. "I can't explain it. And there's probably no use in asking. The Amish don't generally explain to outsiders their reasons for doing things."

"I've gathered that." Fiona's mind flickered to that disturbing conversation with Ted after Rachel's visit.

If Ted was trying to help her understand, he wasn't doing a very good job of it. Maybe his own emotions were getting in the way. After what Rachel had said about Ted courting her aunt, she could understand why he'd have strong feelings on the subject.

But she wasn't going to discuss that with Nolie.

"Anyway, I was glad to see the carpenters back at work today. And for Ruth's sake, I was happy to see the quilters back in the general store. I'd hate to cause problems for her."

Nolie nodded. "I've heard about her store. I understand she gets orders from all over the country for those handmade quilts." She glanced toward the back of the station wagon, piled high with packages. "Speaking of buying and selling, we did pretty well today, didn't we?"

"We did. I can't thank you enough. I'd never have found all those outlets alone." Thanks to Nolie's expertise, she'd found most of the curtains and linens she needed for the house and her practice at bargain prices.

"It was fun." Nolie shot her an amused glance. "Much more fun than shopping with Gabe, believe me. All he ever says is, 'It looks fine. Are you done now?'"

"I can imagine." She smiled, but a thread of worry still laced through her mind. "I just hope I'm going to need all these things. What if the Amish decide not to use my services? That would really make a dent in my practice."

"That's not going to happen," Nolie said comfortingly. "But even if it did, I'm sure there are plenty of other moms who'd choose to have midwife care. And you still have your work at the birthing center in Suffolk, too."

"Only two days a week." That was all the birthing center needed of her. At first she'd been delighted. Affiliating with them gave her the backup she needed while allowing her the time to build her own practice.

Now that two-day-a-week paycheck was starting to look pretty small.

"I wouldn't worry too much." Nolie hesitated for a moment. "You know, I've felt from the beginning that God had a specific purpose in bringing you here. I hope you don't mind my saying that."

"No, not at all." A lump formed in her throat. "It's what I've felt, too. But sometimes it's hard to see how it's working out."

Nolie smiled. "Walk by faith, not by sight. That's all any of us can do." She pulled up in front of Fiona's house. "Can I help you carry the packages in?"

"I'll get them. I know you're eager to get home to Gabe and the baby." She leaned across the seat to give Nolie a quick hug. "Thanks. For more than just the shopping."

"Anytime." Nolie's return hug was warm. "What are cousins for?"

Fiona unloaded her purchases onto the porch and waved as Nolie drove away. She and Nolie had moved from being unknown relatives to being friends, and that was certainly a blessing for this day.

She carried one load inside, startled to hear the sound of hammers from the office. She'd thought the carpenters had gone for the day. Dropping the packages at the foot of the stairs, she headed for the office.

And stopped dead in the doorway. One man, Amish by his clothing, knelt to hammer a shelf into place. The person holding the shelf was Ted.

"I didn't realize you were still here."

They both looked up at the sound of her voice, two pairs of nearly identical blue eyes staring at her. Then Ted rose, dusting off his hands.

"Jacob stayed to finish up the shelves." He darted a quick glance around the office. "He thought you might want to start putting things in here."

"That's very thoughtful." Her voice sounded stilted, but she couldn't seem to help it. "Are you helping him?"

What are you doing here? That was what she wanted to say, but she'd already created enough waves in this small community without starting a fresh argument with its only full-time police officer.

The carpenter stood, putting his hammer into a wooden toolbox. "Not so much help," he said, his eyes twinkling. "Ted is good enough for holding things while I work, but if I turned him loose with a hammer, you might be finding your books sliding off the shelf."

Ted's face relaxed in a smile. "If that's so, then you're to blame. You taught me whatever I know about carpentry." He looked at Fiona, and she caught the slight wariness in his eyes. "This is Jacob Rittenhouse. My brother."

She could only hope the shock she felt wasn't reflected in her face. She managed what she hoped was a credible smile. "It's nice to meet you, Jacob. You've done a wonderful job on those shelves."

He ducked his head gravely. "They will be useful."

She'd already noticed that the Amish responded that way. They stressed the usefulness of an object, but the shelves really were a work of art, each rounded edge finished perfectly by hand.

"It's obvious that nothing will slide off any shelves that you make."

He didn't respond to that, as if to recognize the compliment could be construed as bragging. "I will be on my way, now." He started toward the door, pausing long enough to say something in dialect to Ted.

Ted grinned, clapping him on the shoulder, and answered in kind. Then he turned to her, apparently feeling the byplay needed an explanation. "He's warning me not to touch his tools. He's been saying that to me since I was three."

"Because you dropped the bow saw down the well and we were half the day getting it out again." Jacob settled his straw hat more firmly on his head. "You will come to dinner one night soon."

"Soon." Ted followed him out to the porch, saying a few more words she couldn't understand.

Fiona stood where she was, trying to wrap her mind around this. Ted Rittenhouse had been born Amish, obviously. Just as obviously, he was one no longer. How did that fit into the warnings he'd given her about not seeking any relationship with her mother's family?

The screen door creaked. Ted stopped with the door half open. "May I come back in for a moment?"

She nodded. What would he do if she asked the questions that were battering at her mind? Walk away again? That seemed to be his usual response.

"That's really your brother?" The words were out before she had time to censor them. But why should she? He was the one who'd opened the subject of his family background, just by being here with Jacob.

"Yes."

"Just yes? You didn't come back in to satisfy my curiosity?"

"No." His brows drew together. "I came back because I wanted to apologize. What I said about your parents, after Rachel left—I shouldn't have. It wasn't my place to say anything about them."

"I agree. It wasn't." She stared at him, trying to understand what had driven this apology.

"I'm sorry. Can't you just accept that and let it go?" Exasperation edged his voice, and she was tempted to tell him that he wasn't really very good at apologizing.

"No, I can't." She took a breath. Maybe it wasn't wise, but this had to be said. "Because how you react to me has an effect on my acceptance here. And it's really not fair if you're prejudiced against me because my mother left the Amish community, when it's clear that you did exactly the same thing."

Chapter Five

Ted stood where he was for a moment, fighting the urge to turn and walk right out the door. And an almost equally strong urge to take Fiona by the shoulders and make her listen to common sense about dealing with people she didn't understand.

But he couldn't do either of those things. He couldn't walk away, because he was honest enough to recognize the truth in what she said. And he couldn't touch her, because—well, it was better if he didn't explore the possibility of touching her.

She was right in one sense. His attitude toward her was tainted by his past. Neither of them could help that. Maybe that meant she had the right to know a bit more of the truth, if for no other reason than to keep her from stumbling around and causing more trouble by asking the wrong person.

Fiona still waited, her arms folded, face closed off to

him. She had that rare ability to wait, her silence demanding answers.

He moved closer, resting his hand on the carved newel post. The smooth grain of the oak felt warm under his fingers. "The builders did some fine work in this house. Jacob's work will be up to theirs."

"I know." She gave a short nod. "I've seen your brother's skill."

"You want to know." He shrugged. "I guess it's inevitable. Why does Jacob Rittenhouse, Amish carpenter, have a brother who's a police officer?"

Her hands, which had been pressing stiffly against the sides of her navy slacks, relaxed a bit. "It does seem an odd combination."

"I guess it does." He smoothed his palm over the smooth round ball that topped the newel post. The carpenter was long dead, probably, but his craftsmanship lived on. "Folks here in Crossroads know all about me."

"But an outsider like me doesn't."

He studied her for a moment. That almost-red hair came from her Irish relatives, probably. But her skin was the same creamy ivory as Rachel's, and those clear gray eyes turned up here and there in the Stolzfus family and their kin.

"You're not really an outsider, are you? Like it or not, you have ties here." He shrugged. "It's not a very exciting story. You might be bored."

Her mouth softened, and she took a step toward him. "I won't be bored."

"Well, then." How to explain this so that Fiona, who'd probably always had every choice in the world, would understand? "I grew up on a farm not far from here. My brother Daniel and his family run it now." He smiled. "If you want to know what I was like, just go out and look at Daniel's kids—barefoot towheads learning how to care for the stock and harrow the fields. That was me."

"But you weren't just like them. Or you wouldn't be wearing this." She was close enough now to reach out and touch the police patch on his sleeve.

"My mother always said I was born asking why. I suppose that was the first sign. By the time I was a teenager, I was always restless." Maybe he still was, still trying to be sure of his place in the world. "Didn't you ever feel that, even with a warm, loving family behind you?"

Some emotion he couldn't identify crossed her face and was gone. "Not exactly." She shook her head. "We were talking about you, not me."

What was there in his comment to raise her hackles? He didn't know, but he wanted to.

"I was the kid who was always looking over the pasture fence, wondering what was on the outside."

She nodded, gray eyes thoughtful. "I can see that. But why a cop, of all things?"

"That was Bill's fault." He smiled. "Bill Brinks. State Trooper assigned to this area. He had a soft spot for the Amish kids. He'd follow the buggies home on dark nights, when maybe someone had been having a wild rumspringa."

"Someone like you, for instance?" Her lips curved.

"Guilty," he said, trying not to imagine how those lips would feel against his. "My mother says I gave her more gray hairs than all my brothers put together."

Her eyebrows lifted. "I can imagine that."

"Anyway, Bill went from being an interfering nuisance to being a mentor. My family liked him, but they didn't like where my friendship with him was leading me. Away from them. I suppose your family would have felt the same in that situation." He said it deliberately, watching for her reaction this time.

The reaction was there, quick but unmistakable. Odd. He could guess what kind of family life the Flanagans he'd met would have—warm, loving, nosy, interfering. Like Amish Irish. But apparently that wasn't what Fiona's family life had been like.

"So you left home to become a cop."

He nodded. "I left the community before I was baptized into the church, so I wasn't breaking any vows by the actions I took."

Should he remind her that her mother had done the same? Maybe not. She didn't need the reminder.

"You didn't go into the state police, like your friend," she said.

"I was too young, then, and I wanted to see a little of the world. I went to Chicago, worked, finished my education, eventually went to the police academy there."

She looked at him with a bit of skepticism in her face, as if trying to picture him as a big-city cop and having trouble doing so. "Obviously you didn't stay. What made you decide to leave?"

Everything in him hardened against her at that. No one here would tell her, and he wouldn't, either. "Just got to longing for the rural life again. So here I am."

"And they welcomed you back."

No wonder she sounded skeptical. The Stolzfus family hadn't exactly welcomed her.

"They did. They don't understand my choice, and they have a lot of trouble seeing me wear a gun, but they accept me." He took a step closer to her, close enough to see the tiny blue highlights in the gray of her eyes. "You see, I know how much pain it causes an Amish family when a child leaves. I know, because I did it."

Her gaze evaded his. "But—children do leave home. It's natural, isn't it?"

"It's natural for the world. Not for the Amish."

Her head came up. "It's not my fault that my mother made the choice she did."

"I know that. They do, too. All I'm saying is—"

What was he saying? What did he hope to gain by telling his story to this outsider?

But she wasn't an outsider, not really. And she was hurting. He could see beyond her brave facade. He knew she was hurting, probably more than she wanted to admit.

"Just be patient." He forced a smile. "Maybe, in time, your mother's family will come to terms with Hannah's choice, like mine did."

Her eyebrows lifted. "Didn't you leave a little something out of your story?"

"I left a lot out." His mind flickered to the pain of those last months in Chicago, and he pushed the thought away. "Most of it pretty boring."

"What about your relationship with my aunt Emma? That's kind of pertinent, isn't it?"

"Rachel told you." He traded annoyance for resignation. Young Rachel bubbled on like a brook, and there was no changing that.

She nodded. "I thought maybe—" She stopped, as if reluctant to voice what she thought.

"You thought my attitude toward you was affected by my courting Emma." He shrugged. "Well, maybe it was, but not in the way you think."

"You don't know what I think." She rushed the words.

He couldn't suppress a smile, thinking of Fiona's younger self. "I was sixteen, maybe seventeen. Emma was the same. She was my first love."

"They say you never forget your first love," she said.

"They say?" He raised an eyebrow. "What about you? Have you forgotten your first love?"

A faint flush bloomed like a rose. "We weren't talking about me." Her eyes slid away from his.

Well. That was an interesting response from a woman her age, he'd think.

"I guess we weren't. Well, I was already planning on leaving, and like any young fool in love, I wanted Emma to say she'd go with me."

"She refused to leave her family?"

"She refused. Smartest thing she could have done. We weren't anywhere near ready for marriage." He'd still rushed away in anger and hurt. "But we didn't see that then, and she stayed because of her mother."

Fiona instinctively moved her hands, as if to push him away. He met her gaze and held it.

"She'd been a small child at the time, but she remembered what happened when Hannah left. She remembered that their mother seemed to turn into an old woman overnight. She remembered the pain that she felt nearly killed her mother. And she wouldn't go with me, because she couldn't subject her parents to that pain again."

Fiona's face whitened, her gray eyes looking very dark. "It wasn't my fault." It was a whisper.

"No, it wasn't." Sympathy for her flooded him. "I'm not saying it to hurt you, Fiona. I'm not blaming you for anything that happened to Emma and me. It was for the best. She has a happy marriage, and I have the career I want. We're friends. But the family—well, now you know how they were hurt when your mother left."

"Now I know," she repeated, looking as if the words were acid in her mouth.

"Just tread carefully where the family is concerned. For your sake, as well as theirs."

He touched her then, gripping her shoulder in what he meant to be an encouraging gesture. He wasn't ready for the warmth that surged through him from that touch.

It was as if they were connected by a current that flowed back and forth between them, binding them together.

He let go, his mind scrambling for something coherent to say. There wasn't anything. But it was very clear that Fiona wasn't the only one who'd better be careful.

"Aunt Siobhan, that sandwich tray is beautiful." Fiona shook her head at the array of food that her Flanagan relatives were piling on her kitchen table and counters. "This is too much. I didn't expect you to do all this."

Her aunt paused in the act of sorting cookies onto a serving tray, glancing at her with something like surprise in the deep-blue eyes that were so like Gabe's. "Well, of course we want to help, Fiona. That's what family is for."

Something grabbed Fiona's heart, making her momentarily speechless. Maybe Aunt Siobhan realized it, because she left the cookies and came to give Fiona a quick hug, her movements as light and supple as a girl's.

"We love being part of your open house, dear." She pressed her cheek against Fiona's. "You wouldn't take that away from us, would you?"

"Just be happy the men aren't here." Mary Kate, Aunt Siobhan's older daughter, pushed her way through the screen door, balancing a large white box filled with cupcakes. "You don't know how they can eat. There'd be nothing left for your prospective mothers."

"It won't just be moms," Fiona said. She took the box, sliding it onto the counter. "Although I'm hoping for a good turnout of possible clients." And praying. "I've invited the whole township, it seems. You never know who might be in a position to refer a pregnant woman."

"Good business," Mary Kate said approvingly, running a hand through curls so deep a red they were almost mahogany. Those came from the Flanagan side of the family, and Mary Kate's two kids had inherited the red curls, too.

"It was nice of you to come. I hope you didn't have to hire a sitter." She said the words tentatively, knowing Mary Kate's husband had died about a year earlier, not sure how she managed with two young children, and a burgeoning career as a physical therapist.

"The kids are busy pestering Grandpa this afternoon." Mary Kate smiled. "And I'm happy to have some girl-time, even if I'm not a prospective client."

Something seemed to shadow Mary Kate's face at that. Regret, perhaps? She was still young, still capable of falling in love again, having more children.

The door swung again, and Nolie came in with Terry, the younger Flanagan daughter who'd followed her father and brothers into firefighting but had gone on to become a paramedic. The kitchen was suddenly filled with laughter and female voices, and a warmth she hadn't known she was missing flooded Fiona.

This was how a kitchen should be. Filled with the pleasure that came of working together with family— of having people who accepted her and shared her aims just because they were hers.

Even if they didn't approve, as in Ted's case. His family accepted him back, even though they could never accept the gun and badge he wore.

"Have you seen Ted Rittenhouse lately?" Nolie asked, as if she'd been reading her thoughts.

"Not in a few days, at least not to talk to." Ten days, but who was counting? She'd thought he might turn up again to help Jacob with the carpentry, but he hadn't, and that job was finished now.

"He seems like a nice guy, from what Gabe said." Nolie filled a tray with cupcakes. She paused, pulling one from the tray and handing it to Mary Kate. "This one looks as if someone's little finger got into the icing."

"I guess you'll have to eat it, Mary Kate." Fiona could only be glad that Mary Kate's child's indiscretion took the conversation away from the subject of Ted.

The others began teasing Mary Kate about her having to eat any cakes with fingerprints, and Fiona escaped with a tray into what she'd begun calling the "group room," where she hoped she might eventually hold birthing classes. At the moment, it had two long, covered tables—one for food, the other divided between a coffee and tea station and rows of booklets and materials about midwifery to give out to anyone who was interested.

The questions about Ted had unsettled her, and she tried to push them away. Ted's social life was no concern of hers. She had no idea what he did during his free hours. He might be going out on dates every night of the week, for all she knew.

Not with her. After that revelation about the end of his relationship with Emma, she understood his attitude toward her a lot better. But the attraction was there—they both recognized that, even if they had no intention of admitting it.

Her mother's actions had, however inadvertently, ruined his love for Emma. Maybe it was just as well, maybe they'd been too young, maybe it would have ended as unhappily as her parents' marriage had. Still, he had to find her a reminder.

She'd known he found her presence painful for his friends. Now she realized that it might be painful personally, as well. No one could blame him for steering clear of her. No one.

"Your first visitors are gathering on the porch." Aunt Siobhan hurried in, followed by the others, bearing more trays of food. "Go on, dear, and welcome them. We'll see that everything is set up properly here."

Fiona nodded. She should thank them again, but a flock of butterflies seemed to be fluttering around her stomach, and her throat had closed. Pinning a smile to her face, she hurried to the door to open it officially for the first time.

An hour later she was taking a breather after having given her hundredth introductory spiel when Nolie shoved an oatmeal cookie into her hand.

"Relax and eat something. Enjoy." She grinned. "You're a success."

"I guess so." She looked around at the rooms, still crowded with people. "Are you sure they're not just here for the free refreshments?"

"Look at them. Every person is holding some of your brochures. If they're not going to be clients themselves, they'll tell someone else. It may take time and patience, but this is going to work."

"Patience is a given in the midwifery field. Babies seldom arrive when expected." She glanced around again. There were several young women who might be in need of her services, but none in Amish garb. "I'd hoped for some sign of acceptance from the Amish today."

Nolie poked her. "Well, then, you have it. Look who's coming in."

Pleasure flooded Fiona, and she hurried toward the three women in the doorway—Susie, Aaron's wife, obviously blooming with pregnancy, along with two other young Amish women. Ridiculous, to be so elated at the sight of them.

"Susie, I'm so happy you're here."

"I wanted to see your office, even though my baby will be born at home." Susie patted her rounded belly, and then she nodded to the young woman on her left. "This is my friend, Miriam Hostetler. She wants you to deliver her baby. And her sister, Elizabeth. Elizabeth's father planted a whole row of celery in the garden this year, so we think a wedding will be announced soon." Fiona looked at her, puzzled. Celery?

The younger woman blushed, nodding. Miriam said

something to her and then smiled at Fiona. "Celery is an important part of the wedding feast. We say you can tell when a daughter will be married by the amount of celery in the garden."

"Well, I'm happy to meet both of you. Miriam, if you'd like to make an appointment, I can come to your home, or you can meet me here." She gestured toward the door to the meeting room. "Why don't you go in and have some refreshments now, and we'll talk later."

They nodded, moving off in a group. She couldn't control the elation that bubbled through her. This day was a success, wasn't it?

She glanced toward the door, saw who stood there, and swallowed hard. She really shouldn't feel that rush of pleasure at the sight of Ted's tall figure. He hovered awkwardly on the doorstep, as if unsure of his welcome.

She smiled at him. "Please, come in. The open house is for everyone, not just expectant mothers."

He stepped inside, holding out something in a soft cloth. "I brought you a little housewarming gift. Sorry it's not wrapped fancy, like some of those."

He glanced at the hall table that overflowed with everything from homemade jelly to houseplants.

"You didn't need to bring anything." She took the bundle, her fingers brushing his as she did. "I didn't expect gifts from anyone."

"Folks around here like to say welcome," he said. "Open it."

She opened the cloth, exposing what it hid. The plaque was of wood, not brass, but otherwise it was exactly as she'd envisioned it that first night when she'd looked at the house: Fiona Flanagan, Nurse-Midwife.

Her throat choked. "Thank you." She managed to stammer the words. "And thank Jacob." For surely this delicate carving must have come from him.

"Jacob just supervised," he said. "In spite of what my brother might say, I did the work." His fingers brushed hers again. "Welcome to Crossroads, Fiona."

"Thank you." She didn't dare look up at him, because she didn't want him to see the silly tears in her eyes.

He glanced over her shoulder, as if sensing her feelings and trying to spare her embarrassment. "I see Susie brought you some prospective clients."

She nodded, clearing her throat so that she could speak normally. "Only three Amish turned up, but plenty of other people."

"Well, it's a start." His fingers touched hers again as he took the sign. "Would you like me to go and put this up for you?"

"Yes. Thank you." As he said, it was a start.

The auction sign was large, handmade and decorated with a bunch of balloons so that no one could miss the proper turn. Fiona turned her car onto the narrow dirt lane that led between cornfields toward, presumably, the site where she hoped to pick up a few pieces of furniture she needed for the house.

The corn had been left standing in the field. She'd learned enough in her weeks here to know that was unusual. Most of the corn had long since been cut for silage to feed the animals over the winter. Only here did the stalks stand, brown and sere, looking abandoned.

She shook her head. Silly to be thinking such mournful thoughts. Perhaps the farmer and his wife had retired to a well-earned rest in Florida or some other sunbelt state, and the proceeds from the sale of things they'd left behind would pay for new furniture for a bright sunroom or a boat to putter along a warm bay.

She emerged from the cornfields to a busy sight. People thronged over the lawn between house and barn, talking, laughing, acting as if this event was a party. The auctioneer stood beneath a canopy ringed by lawn chairs, already filled. It was probably smart, auction-goers bringing their own chairs with them.

She pulled into a row of cars in a stubbly field and parked, trying to douse a surge of apprehension. She didn't look like any more of an outsider than the yuppie couple climbing out of their big SUV next to her. And if any of her mother's family happened to be here—well, she'd cope with that if it happened.

In the week since the open house, things had settled down to what might be her new normal. Several clients had come to engage her services, including Susie's friend, Miriam Hostetler. Ruth's quilters were back at work, including Emma, but she'd regretfully put the pieces of her mother's quilt away again. Somehow she didn't have the heart to ask anyone else to finish the quilt after what had happened.

She slid out of the car, grabbed her bag and headed for the center of activity. She could hear the auctioneer's chant from here, and she pushed her way through the throng. It would be nice to see someone she knew, although the odds of that probably weren't great. The auction had certainly attracted a mob of people—farmers mixed with smart, young well-dressed couples who'd probably come out from Suffolk for a Saturday of antiquing, together with a scattering of Mennonite and Amish.

Her stomach churned. She looked around, trying to see if any of her mother's family was there. It had to happen sooner or later.

Not today, Lord. Please. I'm not ready.

How often had she said that? She knew, perfectly well, that she'd spent much of her life withdrawing from the chance of emotional hurt. She even knew why. The problem was finding the courage to change.

I know I said I'd be different when I came here, Father. I'll try not to be a turtle, hiding in my shell. I will. I just don't want to face them today.

And what about Ted? Did she want to face him? He'd stopped by the house twice during the week, casually—so casually, in fact, that she couldn't decide whether the visits were a gesture of friendship or what he saw as his duty, checking up on the new resident.

She'd reached the edge of the crowd around the auctioneer, and she peered past bodies to get a look at what he was selling. Farm equipment, apparently. Maybe she'd have time to look over the furniture before he got that far.

She glanced across the crowd. The furniture seemed to be set out on the dry grass on the far side. She took a step in that direction and then stopped. That slim figure, surely, was Emma Brandt, bending over to inspect a marble-topped nightstand.

Without even thinking about it, she turned and walked in the opposite direction, ending up on the edge of the crowd. She faced a garden with pumpkins and winter squash that showed orange and green among the vines.

"Looking for a nice pie pumpkin?"

She knew it was Ted without looking. She turned, managing a smile. There was no point in letting him know she was such a coward.

"Miriam Hostetler told me about the celery in Amish gardens. I was just thinking there's none planted here."

He smiled, face relaxed. He wasn't in uniform today, but his broad shoulders filled out the plaid shirt he wore with jeans and a denim jacket. "Old man Henderson wasn't Amish, and he wasn't marrying off any daughters this November, that's for sure."

"November?"

He nodded. "It'll soon be here. November is the traditional month for Amish weddings, after the harvest is in and before the snow flies. Maybe Miriam told you that they don't announce the wedding until a few weeks ahead, but if a man plants a lot of celery, it means he's thinking of a wedding feast."

"That's what Miriam said."

A silence fell between them, but it seemed a comfortable one. Maybe Ted had gotten past his worries about her presence here. It would be nice to think they could be friends.

Just friends, the cautious side of her added quickly. Just friends.

Suddenly the silence didn't feel so comfortable. "Are you planning to bid on anything today?" she asked.

He shook his head. "Probably not, but I can never resist the lure of an auction. You never know what treasure you might find. How about you?"

"I thought I might pick up a piece of furniture or two for the house. I can't bid on anything very big, or I won't be able to haul it."

He gave her a quizzical look. "The furniture is over on the other side of the tent."

"I know. Unfortunately, so is my aunt Emma. Maybe my grandmother."

She hadn't been able to identify any of the other black-caped figures from this distance, their bonnets and capes making them as anonymous as she'd thought she'd be in this crowd.

"I see." He glanced across the crowd, his height letting him see easily over the heads of most people. "It looks like most of the Stolzfus and Brandt families are here today."

She tried, and failed, to read any emotion in his voice. "Do you think I should leave?"

She could see that he didn't like being put on the spot with the question. She wasn't sure how to read him—his expression didn't change with the question. But she knew. Maybe his square jaw got a little squarer, or maybe she was developing way too much insight where Ted Rittenhouse was concerned.

"No," he said finally. Reluctantly, she thought. "If you're going to live here, they'll have to come to some way of dealing with your presence."

His concern, as always, was for them, not her, but at least he seemed to recognize that they needed to adjust, too.

"There's no 'if' about it. I'm here to stay."

He gave a short nod. "There's your answer, then."

And you regret it, don't you? Maybe she'd better get away from him before she said something like that aloud to him, instead of in the privacy of her mind.

She pulled her corduroy jacket a little closer around her. "I'm going to find some hot coffee. Will you excuse me?" She didn't wait for an answer, but started across the short, crisp grass to the food stand she'd spotted near the barn.

He didn't follow her. Well, she hadn't expected him to. He'd made it clear from the beginning whose side he was on in this standoff with her mother's family. She needn't imagine he'd change because of some vagrant bits of attraction between them.

By the time she reached the food stand, she'd managed to let go of whatever irritation she felt toward

Ted and refocused her attention on what she hoped to buy today. A nightstand would be nice, and she could fit that in the back of the car. She tried to picture how it would look in her bedroom, next to the new bed.

The steaming hot chocolate smelled even better than coffee, and she took a large cup. One sip sent warmth surging through her, chasing away the late-October chill.

She'd just started back around the barn when she heard the sound of rushing feet behind her. Before she could turn they'd raced past her—three or four teenage boys, brushing so close they jostled the cup, splashing hot chocolate over her hand. Judging by the muffled laughter she heard as they disappeared around the barn, that was what they'd intended.

Annoyed, she fumbled in her bag for a tissue to mop the chocolate from her hand and wrist. A splash had hit the sleeve of her jacket, but it wasn't bad. The boys had judged it nicely. They'd bumped her just enough to bother her, but not enough that she'd go seek out the law.

The odd thing was that, although three of the four had been typically clad in jeans and expensive sneakers, their jackets emblazoned with the emblem of the local high school, one, slighter and smaller, had been Amish. That was a strange combination, she would think.

Now she had a soggy tissue, but there was a large plastic trash bin at the corner of the barn. She dropped the tissue in. Well, no harm done. She rounded the corner, still feeling distracted after the odd encounter, barely looking where she was going, and stopped, face-to-face with her aunt Emma and her grandmother.

For an instant they froze, too, obviously just as shocked as she was. Then, with a quick movement, her grandmother turned her face away, the brim of the black bonnet effectively hiding her face. Emma did the same. And they walked off.

Fiona stood stock-still. The spray of hot chocolate had been nothing compared to this. She felt as if she'd just been doused with an entire bucketful of ice water. If she'd wondered how they'd react to seeing her, she certainly knew now.

Chapter Six

Fiona was straightening the exam room after her last appointment of the day when she heard the bell jingle over the front door. Maybe a new client? She walked quickly through to the reception room. Standing uncertainly near the door was Rachel Stolzfus, and behind her was a young Amish boy.

For an instant Fiona felt as she had the previous Saturday at the auction—first icily frozen, and then scalded with hot embarrassment at the public snub. She forced her emotions under control. These were two kids, hardly responsible for what their elders had done.

"Rachel. How nice to see you." She had to tread carefully. "But I suspect you shouldn't be here."

Rachel's pink cheeks turned even pinker, but she shook her head, her bonnet ties fluttering. "No, it is all right, Cousin Fiona. Really." She pulled the boy forward. "This is my little brother, Levi. He is almost thirteen."

Levi looked like every other Amish boy she'd seen—blond hair in a bowl cut under his cap, round blue eyes that stared at her solemnly, rosy cheeks, and clothes that were a smaller replica of what his father would wear. He looked younger than the average twelve-year-old, but that was probably the inevitable difference in clothes and hairstyle.

"Hi, Levi. It's good to meet you." Fiona smiled at them.

He nodded, not speaking, and his gaze swept around the room, taking in the braided rug on the floor, the straight-backed, padded chairs, racks of mother-to-be magazines and the small television that played quietly in the corner.

Well, maybe it was better not to give him too much attention. Levi was obviously shy of his strange new cousin, and Rachel had probably dragged him along on this visit. Fiona turned back to the girl.

"Are you sure you should be here? I don't want to get you into any trouble."

But Rachel was already shaking her head again. "Aunt Emma brought us with her. She has some work to do at Ruth's. She told us she would be busy for an hour, and we should find something to do. She knew we would come here." Rachel beamed. "So, you see, it makes no trouble."

In other words, Emma had given the kids tacit approval to do what she wouldn't. Or couldn't. Fiona wasn't sure how she felt about that, but again, she couldn't take that out on the kids.

She slipped out of her lab coat and hung it on the coatrack. "Come back to the kitchen. I think it's about time for a snack."

Levi glanced from the television to Rachel. She shook her head.

"Levi would like to stay here and watch the television, if that's all right, while we have a sit-down talk."

"That's fine." She didn't suppose a half hour of daytime television could do him much harm, and the game show that was on seemed fairly innocuous.

She led the way back to the kitchen, taking a mental inventory of her snack provisions. Probably not much there that would appeal to them.

"How about a peanut butter and jelly sandwich?" She glanced at Rachel. "I haven't had a chance to get to the store lately."

"Levi would love it." Rachel took her bonnet off and patted her hair. "Maybe you and I would share one?"

"That sounds good."

Fiona got the makings out quickly, slicing the loaf of brown bread that one of today's clients had brought and getting out the peanut butter and a jar of strawberry preserves Miriam had given her. One thing about working here—she certainly wasn't going to starve, with all the gifts of food that were being pressed on her.

Rachel took the plate with one sandwich from her hand. "I will take it to Levi."

Wondering a bit, Fiona looked after the girl as she

slipped out of the kitchen. It seemed fairly obvious that Rachel wanted a private talk. But about what?

Rachel was back quickly, sliding into the chair opposite Fiona at the round kitchen table. Her spotless apron and deep cherry-colored dress seemed to fit well with the simple aspect of the pine table.

"This is nice, Cousin Fiona."

"Yes, it is." And what is on your agenda, Rachel?

Rachel stared down at the sandwich, not eating it. "Cousin Fiona, will you tell me something?"

"If I can," she replied, wary of promising anything she might not be able to deliver.

Rachel's gaze met hers. "Will you tell me how your mother died?"

For a moment Fiona couldn't speak. That was certainly the last question she'd expected from her young cousin. She swallowed hard.

"Doesn't the family know that?"

Rachel shook her head. "Only that she is dead. That was all my grandfather ever heard about her after she left Crossroads."

She blinked. "But he could have found out more. If he'd wanted to know."

Bitterness twisted. He could have found out about me, that was what she really wanted to say.

"That is not the Amish way, you see. Accept what happens as God's will. Don't question. That is our belief."

"But you do question, don't you, Rachel?" She'd glimpsed a bright, inquiring mind in this young cousin.

Rachel shrugged. "I try not to. But I see our grandmother's sorrow, and I wonder if it might have been eased if she'd known more."

"Maybe you're right." She took a breath to release the tightness is her throat. "My father only ever told me that my mother died after I was born. When I was old enough, I found out more for myself."

"You needed to know," Rachel said.

She nodded, trying to frame the words. This was harder than she'd thought. "Apparently she never adjusted to being away from here. She was sad, crying a lot. After I was born, she developed an infection while she was still in the hospital. The doctor I spoke with said that she just seemed to give up. I guess she didn't want to live."

Even for me, the little voice in the back of her mind said. Even for me.

Rachel's warm, strong fingers wrapped around hers. "I'm sorry. Sorry that you never knew her. That your father had all the care of you."

She shook her head. "My father couldn't take care of me. He put me in foster care."

"Foster care." Rachel frowned. "That is when a relative takes care of the children if the parents can't."

Maybe in Rachel's world that was what happened. "We didn't have any relatives in California. I was placed with strangers, not family."

Judging from Rachel's expression, that concept was beyond her understanding. Her blue eyes were wide, protesting.

"I was well taken care of," she went on quickly. "After my father remarried, I went to live with him."

"And then you were happy." Rachel obviously wanted a happy ending to the story. "You have brothers and sisters, a real family of your own."

The innocent words hurt, but she wouldn't let Rachel see that. "One brother, two sisters. They're quite a bit younger than I."

Rachel nodded sagely. "I know what that is like. Levi, he wishes to follow me everywhere, as if it is time for his rumspringa, not mine."

Fiona smiled, relieved the subject had moved away from her parents. "He probably envies you."

"He must wait until he is older." Rachel sounded severe. "He doesn't yet have good judgment to make decisions." Her smile sparkled suddenly. "Tell me about college. You went to college, yes?"

"Yes. I went to college to study nursing. And after that, to become a midwife. It was hard work, but fun, too."

"You lived in a dormitory, with other girls, and went out on dates." Rachel happily constructed the life she thought Fiona should have had. "And you have traveled?"

She opened her mouth to talk about her summer at a mission in South America and closed it again, remembering Ted's misgivings about exposing Rachel to the outer world. It wasn't her place to make Rachel long for a different life, even if it might seem natural to her.

Natural to her, yes. But would such a life really be any happier? She didn't know the answer to that.

"A little," she said evasively. "Mostly I studied. And then I worked at a birthing clinic in San Francisco before I came here."

Rachel nodded. "I understand. You became a midwife because of what happened to Hannah."

"I—I don't know." She didn't. She'd have said she barely thought of the mother she'd never known, but maybe the longing had been lurking in her heart all the time. "Tell me, is our grandmother all right?"

Rachel gazed down at the table. "I think she is. But I heard my father and mother talk of the time after Hannah left, when she lay on her bed and cried until my grandfather took her to the special doctor in Suffolk and she had to be in the hospital for a long time."

Here was something she hadn't imagined. So, her grandmother had had a depression severe enough to require hospitalization. Maybe their grandfather feared that Fiona's appearance might cause a recurrence.

Rachel glanced at the clock over the stove and exclaimed something in German, jumping to her feet. "We are past our time. We must meet Aunt Emma."

She whirled, enveloping Fiona in a quick, hard hug before rushing out to the other room and calling Levi's name.

Fiona followed, but they were already out the door by the time she got there. She stared absently at the cartoon on the television and the empty plate on the coffee table.

Rachel had come looking for answers to satisfy her own curiosity about what must seem to her a family secret. She'd left Fiona with enough food for thought to last her a good long time.

Late-afternoon sunlight gave the main street of Crossroads a golden haze. In the distance, Ted could smell a faint whiff of burning leaves, a sure sign of autumn. Crossroads seemed to doze on weekday afternoons, but the weekend would bring its influx of tourists.

And its share of traffic issues. If he was lucky, the only problem would be a fender bender caused by some fool driver gawking at an Amish buggy instead of watching where he was going.

Ted turned into the minuscule office that was all the township could afford for its small police force. If he weren't lucky, the weekend would see more thefts or vandalism. So far the problem had been more annoying than serious, but it rankled that he hadn't been able to lay his hands on the culprits yet. He was here to protect, and he didn't like failure.

At least Fiona no longer seemed to need his help. He didn't begrudge any single moment he'd spent with her, but it was probably best for both of them not to let their friendship become any more than what it was. There were too many complications inherent in that sort of relationship.

He flipped briefly through the report filed by one of his part-time officers. Jerry Fuller aspired to be a big-city detective, and his reports managed to make a lost cat sound like a major felony.

He hadn't seen Fiona since the auction, but he'd heard this and that. Her practice was picking up, apparently, although the Amish hadn't yet fully accepted her. Maybe somebody should have warned her that building a clientele among the Amish took a decade or two.

And her relationship with the Stolzfus family probably complicated matters for her, with people unwilling to take sides between her and her grandparents. He regretted that, but there was nothing he could do. It was past time for him to back off.

He'd just poured himself a mug of coffee when he heard the door open. He swung around to see Fiona standing there, lingering in the doorway as if unsure of her welcome.

He'd have to do something about that rush of pleasure he felt at the sight of her. "Fiona. Come in. Can I help you with something?"

"So this is where you hang out." She glanced around the tiny office, as if interested in the crumbling cork bulletin board that bore community notices and the white board that listed staff assignments. "If you turn around too fast, you'll trip over yourself."

The way she evaded his question told him she did, indeed, want something—something she was reluctant to bring up. Well, that was okay. Plenty of people who came in here just needed a bit of patience to bring out their troubles.

"That's why I try not to make any sudden moves."

He gestured toward his one and only visitor's chair. "Would you like a cup of coffee?"

"No, thanks." She drifted to the white board. "Just how big is the Crossroads police force? I guess a resident like me ought to know that."

"You're looking at the full-time force." He perched on the edge of his desk, bringing himself to her level. "I have two part-time officers now, and usually we add another one in the summer. No dispatcher—if someone calls after I go off-duty, the call comes right to my cell phone."

"In other words, you're never really off duty." She sat, finally, her back very straight.

He shrugged. "That's how I like it."

"It's very different from Chicago." Her gaze slid away from his, as if she regretted expressing so much interest. "You mentioned you'd started in police work there."

"Yes." That came out more abruptly than he meant it to. He didn't care to discuss with Fiona, of all people, why he'd left the Chicago force. "Crossroads police work is different. I suppose it looks like a hayseed operation to you."

Her clear gray eyes widened. "Not at all. I'm impressed that you can manage everything you have to handle. It can't be an accident that this is the most peaceful place I've ever lived."

"Usually." He shrugged, trying not to feel too pleased at her praise. "I wish I could say nothing ever happened here, but then the township wouldn't need me."

"Is there a crime wave going on?" She said it as if the idea were absurd.

He shrugged. "Right now the only pressing cases are a missing dog and a few incidents of vandalism. The dog will probably find his own way home, but I'd love to lay my hands on the vandals before they graduate to something more ambitious than knocking over outhouses."

"I guess I'm lucky I don't have an outhouse." A smile curved her lips at the thought.

He tried to ignore the effect of that smile. "Maybe you're not worried about an outhouse, but you didn't come here just to chat. Not that I don't enjoy it."

The smile slid away. "Yes." She clasped her hands in her lap. "At the auction last Saturday—something happened."

He leaned toward her, elbow on his knee. "Tell me."

"Some boys had jostled me, spilling my hot chocolate. Otherwise I might have been watching where I was going more closely. As it was, I nearly walked into Emma and my grandmother." She took a breath, as if it were difficult to say. "They both turned their heads and walked off as if I weren't even there."

"I'm sorry." He kept the words gentle, sensing the pain the event had caused even though she didn't exactly admit it. "But your grandmother—"

"I know." She looked up, her gaze zoning in on his face. "Rachel came to see me. With, apparently, Emma's tacit approval. She told me about my grandmother's illness."

Was she blaming him for not telling her? He couldn't be sure.

"The family never talks about it," he said.

"Are they ashamed of emotional illness?" Her gray eyes flashed.

"Not ashamed, exactly." How to explain this to an outsider like her? "The Amish way is to accept what happens to you as God's will. Your grandmother wasn't able to accept Hannah's leaving. It took some time for the family to realize that her reaction needed medical intervention."

Pain shadowed Fiona's face. "Rachel said she was hospitalized for a long time."

He nodded, wondering whether she was hurting for her grandmother, her mother or herself. "I don't remember it, but I guess so. I'm sure that's why they're all trying so hard to protect her now."

"You think it's wrong for me to want to see them." Her gaze challenged him.

"Not wrong," he said carefully. "I just think it might be unwise. You have to be cautious."

She surged out of her chair so suddenly that the movement startled him. "Be cautious. Be patient. That's all anyone will say to me."

He rose, playing for time, trying to decide what to say to her. "That's the Amish way."

Her hand slashed, seeming to reject that. "It's just prolonging the agony. Maybe I ought to go out to the farm and confront them."

"No." He hurt for her, even as he worried about the family. "Fiona, you can't do that. If you force the issue, you may never get what you want."

"You don't know what I want." The fire in her was so intense he could feel it. "I'm not sure I do."

He shook his head. "You want to talk to them. Your grandparents. To resolve your feelings."

For a moment longer she glared at him. Then her shoulders sagged, and she shook her head. "I suppose. I've started feeling that I'll never come to terms with the past until I do."

Her eyes met his, and he could see what she was going to ask before the words were out of her mouth.

"Please, Ted. Will you help me? Will you convince them to see me?"

There it was—the straightforward appeal for his help that he'd hoped wouldn't come. He'd never found it easy to say no to someone who needed him. And sometimes it was downright impossible.

He ran his fingers through his hair, wishing he had some magical answer that would make everyone happy. There wasn't one.

"Fiona Flanagan, I knew you were trouble the moment I saw you."

She surveyed him gravely. "Is that a yes or a no?"

"It's a maybe." He shook his head at the hope in her face. He didn't want to respond to that hope. Didn't want to start feeling responsible for her. But it was probably already way too late for that. "Don't build on it too much. But I'll try to think of a way I can help you."

* * *

Taking the black bag that contained everything she needed for a routine prenatal visit, Fiona slid from the car. The Hostetler farm didn't look quite as prosperous as some she'd seen, but Susie's friend, Miriam, had mentioned that she and her husband had just managed to buy it a few months earlier, from an elderly, non-Amish farmer who'd let the place go in recent years.

They'd have a struggle to get the place up to Amish standards, perhaps, but given the price of farmland in the area, they'd been lucky to buy. According to Ruth, many young Amish had left for areas farther north because they couldn't afford land here. Ironic that the presence of the Amish had created the tourism that now threatened their very existence.

Miriam came out onto the porch to greet her, bobbing her head with what seemed a nervous smile. She had the round, rosy cheeks and bright blue eyes of a china doll, but the tension was new since Fiona had met her. Still, first pregnancies could do that—each step in the process could bring up new concerns.

"It's good to see you, Miriam." She smiled reassuringly. "How are you feeling?"

"Fine. I am fine." Miriam gestured to the door. "Please, come in. We must talk."

That worried look wasn't the usual reaction to a prenatal visit, but maybe the young woman had some fears she wanted to be sure she brought up. Fiona followed her into a spotless, sparsely furnished living room.

"Is something worrying you?" Fiona said. "You can talk to me about anything." She set the bag down on the shining wooden floor.

Miriam's cheeks flushed. "It is not that. I wish—I must tell you that I cannot continue to be your patient."

For a moment Fiona could only stare at her. "But I thought we had agreed. If there's some problem with my fee—"

"No, no. It is not that." She paused, fingers twisting together, obviously reluctant to say whatever it was. "It is just that my husband's father, he is second cousin to John Stolzfus. And he thinks—"

She stopped, unwilling or unable to say anything else.

She didn't need to say more. Fiona didn't know whether to laugh or cry.

"Did my grandfather ask you not to see me?"

"Not exactly." Miriam pressed her lips together, shaking her head. "I am sorry. But it would be better if you left now."

She had to take a deep breath and remind herself that the young woman wasn't responsible for this. Miriam would give in to the others' wishes, because that was the Amish way. Fiona managed a smile as she picked up the bag she wasn't going to need.

"It's all right, Miriam. I know it's not your fault." She patted the young woman's arm. "Really. If there's ever anything I can do for you, just let me know."

Miriam nodded, cheeks scarlet.

There wasn't anything else to say, was there? Fiona

kept a faint smile on her lips until she got out the door, though it probably looked more like a grimace. Then she stopped, staring.

Her car still sat where she'd left it, but behind it was the township's black patrol car. Ted leaned against the driver's-side door, but at the sight of her, he pushed away and came toward her.

"Are you following me around?".

The words were snapped in a way Ted didn't deserve. After all, he wasn't to blame, but he was male and he was handy. She stamped down the steps toward her car.

He blinked, but that was the only sign of surprise. His face wasn't made for expressing much emotion, but she'd still learned to read him fairly well.

"No. I'm not following you. Should I have been?"

She tossed her bag into the back seat of the car. "Sorry." She bit off the word. "I shouldn't take my feelings out on you."

"Feel free." He planted one large hand on the door frame. "But you might tell me first what has you so upset."

She'd probably explode if she didn't. "I've just lost a client. Miriam's husband would prefer she didn't see me. And guess why—because his father is my grandfather's second cousin."

"I'm sorry." He shook his head slowly. "I guess this is small consolation, but it's only one client, after all."

She frowned at him, narrowing her eyes against the sun's glare. Around them, fertile fields stretched toward the line of low hills, and a herd of black-and-white cows munched grass in a nearby pasture. It was a tranquil scene, but she didn't feel very peaceful at the moment.

"Clients aren't exactly falling out of the trees for me right now. I can't afford to lose even one. And how many more might I lose if my grandfather has his way?"

Ted studied her with those calm blue eyes that were nearly as placid as the cows' in the face of her annoyance. "Look, you don't know that this was John Stolzfus's idea. It's entirely possible that Miriam's father-in-law is guessing at that, or just wants to stay uninvolved. It doesn't mean your grandfather is trying to undermine your practice."

"Doesn't it?" She stared at him bleakly. He didn't understand. Her bank account was dwindling steadily, and if her practice didn't pick up soon, the likelihood of it surviving a year wasn't very good. "If his influence keeps prospective clients away, it won't really matter whether he told them to stay away or not."

"I'm sure you're tired of hearing this, but you have to give it time. Nothing moves quickly among the Amish." His smile was cautious. "It took two years for the bishop to decide it was all right for an Amish business to have a telephone. Rotary dial, of course."

He obviously hoped to lighten her mood, but it wasn't working.

"Maybe my initial reaction was the right one. Maybe I should just go out and talk to them."

"Don't." He moved then, so quickly that it seemed

his casual attitude was just a pose. His fingers closed around her wrist, as if to emphasize his warning. His hand was warm and strong, and she could feel her pulse accelerate against it.

He must have felt it, too. Almost without her will, her gaze lifted to his. His blue eyes darkened as his pupils dilated, and a current flowed back and forth between them where their skin touched.

They stood motionless, caught in the moment. His muscles tightened, as if he'd pull her against him. She should pull away, but something seemed to push her toward him. The faintest of movements would have her in his arms...

He shook his head, as if surfacing from under water. "I'm sorry." He let go of her wrist slowly. "I know I can't tell you what to do."

He seemed to have trouble getting back to the conversation. She understood. Her heart was beating so loudly she could barely concentrate.

"It's all right." Her voice sounded husky, and she cleared her throat. "You're trying to be fair to everyone. But I just don't know what else to do."

"Maybe there's another way." He shook his head again, as if still trying to clear it. "I wasn't following you today, but I was trying to find you. Ruth mentioned she thought you were coming out here. I talked to Emma." There was the faintest hesitation in his voice as he said her name. "She asked me to tell you she'd like to stop and see you tonight."

Her breath caught. "Did she say why?"

"No, but that's a good sign, isn't it?"

He so obviously wanted to make things right for everyone that it touched her. The big, tough cop had a heart like a marshmallow.

"Maybe." She couldn't allow herself to hope. It wasn't safe to risk her happiness on other people. They so often let her down. She'd learned that before she'd learned to walk. "I guess I won't know until I see her, will I? Did she say what time?"

He shook his head. "Probably whenever she can get free after supper."

"Or when she can make some excuse." It was ridiculous to think that her own aunt had to sneak around in order to visit her.

"At least she's coming." His fingers brushed hers lightly, setting up a tingling that rushed across her skin. "Be happy with that for now. All right?"

"All right." Her fingers brushed his again, in spite of herself. "I'll try."

The flicker of hope she felt startled her. She'd better be more careful. If she spent too much time with Ted, she might actually start to believe in all those old-fashioned things he so obviously valued—things like family loyalty and happily ever after.

Chapter Seven

B y the time she'd wiped the sink for the third time, Fiona had to admit that she was nervous about this impending meeting with her aunt. She glanced out the kitchen window. It was fully dark now, and loneliness seemed to close in on the house as the light went. Surely, if Emma was really coming, she'd be here by now.

Ted had said she would come, and she trusted him. That thought gave her pause. She did trust him. Quite aside from the attraction that flared each time they were together, she liked and trusted him. If he said Emma would be here, then she would.

Crossing quickly to the stove, she turned the gas on under the teakettle. She would treat this visit like a friendly social call, and maybe that's what it would be.

She leaned against the counter, waiting for the kettle to boil, her mind drifting back to those moments with Ted outside Miriam's house. She'd expect, if she were being honest, that it would be that surge of attraction that demanded her attention. Oddly enough, as powerful as that attraction had been, she found herself returning again and again to the sense of concern that had flowed from Ted.

He had cared that she was hurting. His sympathy had been the real thing, not some facile expression. He wanted to make things right for her, and that was stronger than any mere attraction could have been.

Her fingers curled against the edge of the countertop. Other people here cared about what happened to her— the Flanagans, maybe even Ruth and Susie. And she'd let them in—she'd started feeling for them in return.

That wasn't her way. She'd learned as a child that the best way to protect herself was not to open herself. Then it didn't hurt so much to be shipped off to another foster home at a moment's notice, or to sense that she was the outsider in her father's house.

The old ways of protecting herself didn't seem to be working since she'd come here, but she didn't know how else to respond. Apprehension shivered through her. What if she opened herself up to these people and got kicked in the teeth for her trouble? How would she deal with that?

A knock stopped the downward spiral of her emotions. Rubbing her palms against her jeans, she went to open the door.

Emma gave a quick glance back over her shoulder as she stepped inside, but nothing was in the alley between the buildings but her buggy.

"Fiona, I am happy to see you." She shed her

bonnet and cloak, revealing the simple dark dress and apron she always wore. "I am sorry if you have been waiting too long."

"Not at all." Fiona hung the cloak over the back of a chair. The kettle whistled, and she turned to pull it off the burner. "Will you have a cup of tea? Peppermint or Earl Grey?"

"Peppermint, that sounds good."

Fiona poured the tea, then lifted the tray on which she had the mugs ready, along with a small plate of poppy-seed bread that Ruth had brought over earlier. "Let's go upstairs to my living room."

She'd half expected Emma to protest that she couldn't stay long, since that seemed to be the pattern with any Amish visitors, but Emma nodded. She followed Fiona up the back staircase, her long dress rustling.

"This is nice, having the stairs that come right down to your kitchen. Saves time and steps, ja?"

"Yes, it does." She led the way into the living room, where the lamps were already on, bathing the room in their soft glow. "I haven't quite finished with the painting up here yet, but the room is livable, at least."

She was nervous, and that was making her babble. What had brought Emma here tonight? Surely she risked getting into trouble with her parents if they found out.

Emma sat on the sofa, looking around with frank curiosity as she picked up the steaming mug. "This is very nice." She fingered the afghan that was draped over the back of the sofa. "This is Elsie Schuler's work."

Fiona had to smile, despite the tension that skittered along her skin. "If I'd known how recognizable handwork is to you, I probably wouldn't have shown you my mother's quilt pieces."

"The quilt squares." Emma gave a quick, characteristic nod. "I would like to see again."

That startled her. She'd have thought Emma would be happy to forget about them.

Fiona crossed to the bookcase and picked up the small dower chest, carrying it across to Emma. "Maybe you recognize the box, as well."

Emma took it, holding it at eye level for a moment, her eyes bright. "I know it. Our papa, he made one for each of the girls. Mine will go to my daughter one day." She sat the box in her lap, her fingers caressing it. "He made these with much love."

For Hannah, Fiona reminded herself. Not for the granddaughter he didn't want to know. Still, that love seemed to show in the precise corners and delicate painting, even after all this time.

Emma opened the lid carefully and lifted out the quilt pieces. She saw what was underneath and hesitated for a moment before picking up the cap and apron. Her eyes flickered. "So many years. I miss her still, my big sister."

Fiona's heart clenched. "I didn't think about that. I'm sorry."

"It is not your fault. The memories are good ones." She fingered the delicate baby gown. "She made this for you."

"I suppose she did." Tears stung her eyes, and she

blinked them back. "Why did you want to see the quilt patches again?"

Hannah set the box on the coffee table and turned the fabric squares over in her hands. "If you still want, I will make the quilt for you."

"Yes, of course I want. But your mother—"

"I will do it at Ruth's. No one will say anything to my mother about it." Her gaze met Fiona's and slipped away. "You understand, about her illness."

"I know that you're trying to protect her. I don't want to do anything to upset that." Her heart twisted at the thought that her grandmother had to be protected from her existence.

"She won't know," Emma repeated. She smoothed the squares with gentle fingers. "When I was very young, I had a doll, and a tiny cradle my father had made. Hannah—she was one of the grown-ups to me, because she was so much older. But she made a little quilt for the doll cradle." Her smile was soft. "So I will piece the quilt for you, and think of her."

Fiona's throat was too tight for words. She reached toward Emma, barely knowing that she was doing it, and Emma clasped her hand in a hard grip. Fiona couldn't be sure whether the tears that splashed on their hands were hers or Emma's, but they were melting the shell that protected her heart.

Much later that night, Fiona sat cross-legged on her bed, the dower chest open in front of her. Carefully she folded the tiny baby dress and tucked it inside, then the apron, and finally the cap.

She closed the lid, letting her fingers stroke the painted designs. Her grandfather had made this for his firstborn child. It didn't take a lot of imagination to picture the love in his face—after all, she'd seen fathers catching their first glimpse of a son or daughter.

Her heart was so full her chest seemed to ache with it. Another image filled her mind. Her mother, a blond, rosy-cheeked teenager, sat making a doll quilt for her little sister, sewing love into every stitch.

Had she felt that love when she'd sewn the tiny dress for her unborn child? Or had it been overshadowed by her sense of being a stranger in a strange land?

Tears spilled over onto her cheeks, and she wiped them away with her fingers. It was too late now, wasn't it, to cry for her mother? To long for something she'd never known?

Through the blur of tears, she saw her past more clearly than she ever had. When she'd gone to live with her father and her stepmother, she'd known that they didn't welcome questions about her mother. If she'd been a different kind of child, the kind who demanded answers, perhaps things would have turned out differently.

She swung off the bed in a quick movement and put the dower chest on her dresser. She was being foolish, crying over something that was long past. She'd go to bed, and things would look better in the morning.

But even when she'd turned off the lights and curled up in bed, her busy mind wouldn't shut down. She stared at the ceiling, where a faint light reflected from Ruth's store next door, facing the thought that had nibbled at the edges of her mind for days.

Her father hadn't had to put her in foster care with strangers. He could have sent her back to Pennsylvania after her mother died, even if he hadn't wanted to return himself.

The Flanagans would have taken her in, no matter what the quarrel was between her father and her uncle Joe. She'd seen enough of their warm, open hearts to know that.

And her mother's family? Her heart twisted. Would they have taken her in or turned their backs? She didn't know. Maybe she'd never know.

Lord... Her prayer choked on a sob. *I've held back all my life, always afraid of rejection if I got too close. Maybe I've even done the same thing with You. I can't seem to do that any longer, but I'm afraid to change. What if I can't? Please, help me see the way.*

She wiped the tears away again, too tired to get up and do something, too restless to seek refuge in sleep. She stared at the ceiling, trying to sense an answer in her heart. *What...*

Something crossed the rectangle of reflected light on the ceiling. She blinked. What had that been? A bird, maybe, flying between the two buildings—would that cause a shadow like that?

She lay still, watching. In a moment, another shadow crossed the pattern of light, and tension skittered along her skin. That was no bird, or anything else that had reason to be between the buildings or in Ruth's store at this hour of the night. That was a human shape.

Ruth, coming in to do some work? She turned cautiously, as if someone might hear her, looking at the bedside clock. It was hardly likely to be Ruth out and about, not at nearly two in the morning.

She slid out of bed, her bare toes curling into the rag rug, and shivered as she reached for the robe that lay across the footboard. Pulling it around herself, she padded silently toward the window. No one could see her, surely, as long as she didn't turn the light on.

Still, she stood to the side of the window, cold with tension, and peered out cautiously. There was the nearest window of Ruth's store—it was the window of the workroom, where the quilts were. If someone were there on legitimate business, they'd put on a light, wouldn't they? The soft glow was that of the dim light Ruth always left burning in the back room, visible only from the side or the back of the store.

She stood, undecided, clutching the curtain with one hand, her feet cold on the floorboards. She leaned forward, pressing her face against the pane. Her eyes must be growing accustomed to the faint light, because she could make out objects in the narrow passageway between Ruth's store and her house—the old-fashioned rain barrel that stood beneath Ruth's downspout, some boards the carpenters had leaned against the wall.

And a figure. He was mostly in shadow, but she saw the slight movement. On its heels came a sound, the faintest tinkle of breaking glass. Barely audible, it shrilled an alarm in Fiona's mind. The police—she had to call the police.

Afraid to turn on a light, she felt her way across the room and snatched her cell phone from the dresser, taking comfort from its glow. Even as she punched in 911, she remembered what Ted had said. Night calls went directly to him. The thought was oddly reassuring.

"Crossroads police, Ted Rittenhouse here."

She pressed the phone against her ear. "This is Fiona." She kept her voice low. She'd heard the glass break. Could they hear her? "Someone is in Ruth's store. I can see them moving around, and there's a person in the alleyway between her place and mine."

"Stay where you are." His voice was crisp, authoritative. "Are you upstairs? Are your doors locked?"

"Yes. But the store—they're in the quilt room."

"I'm on my way. Don't come out of your house until I tell you it's safe. And don't hang up."

She could hear the sound of the car's motor through the cell phone and realized that he was, literally, on his way.

"Don't worry about me. I'm fine. But all those quilts—"

"Better a quilt than you." He sounded grim. "I'm almost there."

She slid along the wall to the window. "I'm at the upstairs window." A crash interrupted her words, and she realized she was shaking at the violence that implied. In the city it would have sickened but not shocked her—here in this peaceful place it was obscene. "They've knocked something over."

Several things happened at once. She heard, faintly, the sound of a car. The lookout, if that's what he was, must have heard it, too. He moved, rapping sharply at the window frame.

"They've heard you." She rushed the words, as if that would make a difference. "They're coming out the side window, three of them, dark clothes, I can't make out their features. Running toward the back of the building. The other one, the lookout, he's running, too."

Ted muttered something, and then the wail of his siren shattered the night air. Too late now to worry about alerting the intruders. She shoved the window up, leaning out in hope of getting a better view of them.

Their figures were silhouetted briefly as they skirted the light cast by her back porch lamp. Teenagers, she'd guess, by their size and the way they moved. The first three had hoods up, turning them into featureless shapes. The last one—

She pulled back inside so sharply that she struck her head on the window frame, seeing stars for a moment. She sank down on the floor, rubbing her head, the cell phone dropping in her lap.

The last figure—she couldn't be mistaken. The dark

clothes, the shape of the hat, the cut of the trousers—it had been someone in Amish garb.

Ted walked toward Fiona's back door, frustration tightening every muscle. He'd been close, so close. Closer than he'd ever been to catching or at least identifying the vandals, thanks to Fiona, but they'd slipped away again.

He glanced toward the dark patch of woods behind the store. Were they back there someplace, watching him? Common sense said they'd headed straight for home, but he couldn't shake off the thought. What kind of cop couldn't outwit a few teenagers?

No use feeling sorry for his circumstances, because they were his choice. He wasn't a big-city cop anymore, with plenty of backup and a forensic team. He was only one man, and they'd had just enough of a head start to elude him. He could only hope that Fiona had seen something that would help him identify them.

He rapped on the door, frowning at the glass window in it. Very nice to see who was out here, but also very easy for someone to break.

Fiona swung the door open, eyes widening at his expression. "What is it? What's wrong?"

"Nothing. I was just thinking that you should have something more secure for a back door—either a solid door or wire mesh over the window."

She stood back to let him enter the brightly lit

kitchen. A kettle steamed gently on the stove, and the windowsills were bright with pots of yellow mums. "I thought this was a safe place to live."

"So did I." He pulled out his notebook and flipped it open. "Tell me exactly what you saw."

"What about Ruth's store? Have you told her? Did they damage the quilts?"

It was tempting to answer her, to get into a conversation between friends about what had happened, but he couldn't. He needed to get a statement from her as close time wise to the incident as possible so it wouldn't be contaminated in any way by his outside information.

"Concentrate on what you saw and heard." That sounded more abrupt than it needed to. "Please, Fiona. It's important to go over it before you forget."

"I'm not likely to forget." Her voice was tart. She picked up the mug of tea that sat on the table and held it between her hands, as if she needed its warmth. "I couldn't get to sleep, because—well, that doesn't matter."

Because of that visit from Emma? He longed to ask her, but that too would be sidetracking.

She clutched the mug a little more tightly. "The light that Ruth leaves on in the store reflects on my bedroom ceiling. I saw a shadow move across it." She frowned, as if trying to be sure she got it exactly right. "I waited a couple of minutes, thinking maybe it was a bird flying between the buildings, but then I saw it again and knew it was a person. I went to the window."

"Is it possible they could see you?" The last thing either of them needed was for the vandals to target her next.

She shook her head. "I was careful to stay back and leave the lights off." She shut her eyes briefly, as if to visualize what she'd seen. "There were people moving in the store. And there was one outside in the alley, in the shadow of the building."

"People? What kind of people? How many?" His frustration put an edge to his voice.

Her lips tightened. "I'm telling you what I saw then. That was when I called you."

He was ticking her off, apparently. He regretted it, but duty came first. If he'd gotten here a little sooner—but he knew that was impossible. "Did you get a better look at them at any point?"

"The one outside, the lookout, must have heard your car. He said something to them, but I couldn't hear what. Then they all bailed out the window and started running down the alleyway between the buildings."

She came to a stop, but he sensed that there was more. "Your back porch light was on?"

She nodded, glancing toward it.

"Then you must have seen something when they ran past."

"Not much." Her tone was guarded. "The three who had been inside the store ran past first." She frowned a little, shaking her head. "I couldn't get a good look—it happened so fast. They all wore jeans and dark sweatshirts or maybe jackets with the hoods pulled up. Judging by their size and the way they moved, I'd guess they were teenagers, but I can't swear to that." She shrugged. "I'm sorry I can't be more help."

She was holding something back. He knew it, and it angered him.

"This is no time to be evasive. What else did you see? Come on, Fiona, out with it."

"Or what? You'll lock me up?"

"Or you'll be withholding evidence in a criminal case," he replied evenly. "And I know you don't want to do that."

She lifted a hand to her forehead, shoving her hair back, the fight going out of her. "No. Of course not. It's just that I—" She shook her head.

"Whatever it is, it's my job to figure out. Is it something about the fourth boy?"

She nodded. "He was several steps behind the others. When he passed the light I could see—not his face, but his clothing. He was wearing Amish clothing."

It was like a punch to the stomach. For a moment he couldn't say anything at all. Then he shook his head violently. "You must be wrong."

"I know what I saw." Her eyes flashed. "The hat, the dark jacket and pants—believe me, I'd like to be mistaken, but I'm not."

The pain behind her words convinced him. "It's just—" He shrugged, not knowing what to say. "It's unheard of, that's all. Even during their rumspringa, when they have more freedom to try things, Amish youngsters don't get up to criminal mischief, especially not with English teens."

Fiona rubbed the back of her neck tiredly. "I wish I hadn't seen it. But maybe it was some kind of a prank—a kid dressed up in Amish clothing, hoping to throw the blame on them."

"Possible, I suppose, if these kids are cleverer than I've been giving them credit for." Dread was building in him. Balancing between two worlds wasn't an easy thing at the best of times. If he had to arrest an Amish kid, he'd be landing in no-man's-land. "Look, are you sure—?"

"Do you think I like this any better than you do?" Fiona had to be at the end of her rope. "What do you think it will do to my practice with the Amish if word gets out that I'm accusing one of them?" She paled. "Please—this doesn't have to be public, does it? Maybe you can forget who told you."

He stiffened. "I have to do my duty, no matter how little I like it."

"I'm not asking you to break any laws." Her eyes darkened. "But does doing my duty as a citizen have to cost me a big share of my practice? The Amish community is already wary of me."

"I hope not." He shook his head, suddenly bone-tired. "I won't be making anything public while I'm conducting an investigation, but if it comes to an arrest, I can't promise you anything."

She gave a short nod, seeming to pull back into herself. "All right. I guess I can't expect anything else."

His duty stood like a barrier between them, and she must know it as well as he did. Unfortunately, there wasn't a thing he could do about it.

Chapter Eight

"This is going to look terrific." Nolie ran her paint roller over the wall of Fiona's living room, then stood back to admire the effect of the light moss green. "I love to paint. It makes everything look so fresh and new."

"You've come to the right place, then." Fiona divided her smile between Nolie and Aunt Siobhan, both clad in jeans and T-shirts, bandanas protecting their hair. "I can't tell you how much I appreciate your help."

And your support. She wanted to add that, but was still reluctant to expose how much they all meant to her.

"It's a pleasure." Aunt Siobhan, looking as young as one of her daughters in the casual clothes, swept a brush along the woodwork. "And besides, it gives us a chance to catch up with you. How is the practice going? Is it building the way you expected?"

Fiona frowned, watching the dingy tone of the wall disappear with a sweep of the roller. "I'm not sure just what I expected. I'm getting by, so far." She wouldn't tell them how slim her bank account had become. "But the Amish should be a large part of a nurse-midwife practice in this area, and so far that's not happening."

Siobhan's concerned expression seemed to say that she read what wasn't spoken. "You know that you can come to us if you need anything, don't you?"

Her throat tightened. She still wasn't used to the open-handed, open-hearted way these relatives had accepted her. "Thank you, but it hasn't come to that yet."

"Is this reluctance of theirs because of your mother's family? Have you had a chance to talk with them yet?" Nolie's roller moved in time with her question, efficient as always. No wonder she was able to juggle her family and her life-altering work so smoothly.

"I've talked with an aunt and a cousin," she said. "So far my grandparents haven't been willing to see me."

Distress filled Siobhan's eyes. "I'm sorry. That just seems so heartless—"

"It's not that," she said quickly. "I thought that at first, but it seems my grandmother ended up hospitalized with severe depression after my mother left. They're trying to protect her, not hurt me."

"Even so, it affects your livelihood," Nolie said. "It's so unfair."

And now she had that business with the vandals to add to her potential problems. At least according to Ruth, they'd been scared off before they'd done more than tip over a display stand. Even Ruth didn't know her involvement. Ted had said he'd keep her part quiet for the time being, but he clearly wouldn't bend any regulations for her. She'd come up against that rigid cop mentality of his a couple of times, and she didn't like it.

"Is something else wrong?" Siobhan's words were soft, but they pierced Fiona's heart. Her aunt Siobhan just saw much too clearly.

The longing to pour all her worries into her aunt's sympathetic ear almost overwhelmed her. Almost, but not quite. The old habit of holding back, not rocking the boat, was too strong to be overcome that easily.

"No, nothing." She managed a smile. "I guess I just didn't realize how much of an effect my mother's decision would have on me."

"Ripples in a pond," Siobhan said. "We can never know how many people will be affected by the things we do. It wasn't just your mother's decision, you know. Your father's actions caused their own set of problems."

"You mean with his brother?" Was she finally going to learn what the breach between Uncle Joe and her father was all about?

Siobhan's eyes were touched with sadness. "It was a terrible quarrel, terrible. Joe was as much to blame as his brother. He should have known you don't dissuade someone from falling in love by shouting at him."

Her throat tightened. "You mean their breach was caused by my mother?"

Siobhan caught her hand and held it firmly. "No, don't think that. It certainly wasn't your mother's fault.

They fell in love, and the only way Michael could see to deal with the situation was by taking her away. Of course Joe thought they were too young, that Michael was ruining her life, and that he wasn't thinking it through. All that was true enough, but not what Michael wanted to hear.

"I'm so sorry that they've never made it up." Ripples in a pond, indeed.

"Well, what Joe never wanted to admit was that he'd always pictured Michael going into the fire service, as he and their other brother did. That rankled, when Michael was ready to throw that away. And then it turned into plain old Flanagan stubbornness, with neither of them willing to make the first move."

"Flanagans are famous for their stubbornness," Nolie said, bending to put her roller down on the tray. "But this seems over the top, even for a Flanagan."

"Of course it does." Siobhan's tone went brisk with what sounded like exasperation. "The sad part is that say what he will, that stubborn husband of mine will never really be right spiritually until he's forgiven his brother and himself for this foolish quarrel."

"I suppose my being here has only made it worse." Everywhere she turned, it seemed Fiona found more problems generated by her presence.

Siobhan's eyes widened. "If you think that, then I'm telling this all wrong. If not for that stupid quarrel, we'd have known earlier about your mother's death and maybe have been able to help. Your being here is finally making Joe take a long look at his behavior. Mind, I'm not saying he'll jump right in with an apology, but I think he's ready to mend things if your father is." She looked at Fiona expectantly.

Fiona felt helpless. "I don't know," she said. "Really, I don't. My father never talked about his brother, just as he never talked about my mother. I have no idea how he'd react if Uncle Joe called him."

"How did he react to your coming here?" Siobhan asked.

"He didn't like it." She could only hope her voice didn't betray how difficult that had been. She still cringed when she thought of that icy scene. "And it seems unanimous. My grandparents don't like it, either."

Or Ted. But she wasn't going to say that.

Siobhan gave her a hug, heedless of their paint-daubed clothes. "Well, it's not unanimous, because we love having you here. And it will work out with the others, too. You'll see." She kissed Fiona's cheek. "I'm praying for you. God will bring good out of this situation. I know it."

Siobhan's words still comforted her that evening as she turned off the light in the office. She'd sat there after supper, going over the records on her patients, organizing her files. The work comforted her, as Aunt Siobhan's words did. It affirmed who she was.

The difficult moment came when she'd turned off the lights and walked up the stairs, as she was doing now.

This was the lonely time, she had to admit it. Crossroads was so quiet at night, the house incredibly still. Of course she'd rather have it that way than have the excitement of the break-in at Ruth's store.

She was bending over to take a magazine from the basket next to her chair when the phone rang. It was rare enough to hear it that the sound startled her. She picked it up.

"Fiona Flanagan."

"Fiona, I'm glad I caught you." Ted's voice crackled in her ear, and she caught the wail of a siren in the background. "Miriam Hostetler and her husband have been in an accident—a car hit their buggy. The paramedics are on their way, but she's asking for you. Will you come?"

"Of course." A silent prayer for the young woman and her husband filled her mind. "How bad is it?"

"I'd have said not too serious, but she's scared and shaken up and worried about the baby. We're on the road you took to their farm the other day—about three miles past the Amish schoolhouse."

"I'm on my way." She hung up, snatched her handbag and raced down the stairs to pick up her medical kit as she rushed to the car.

She spun out onto the road, mentally rehearsing the way to the farm. It would take just minutes to get there, just time enough to consider the possibilities. It was highly unlikely for an accident to harm the baby at this early stage, as well protected as it was, but she'd learned to listen to the mother's intuition. If Miriam thought something was wrong, she had to take that into account.

Lord, You're seeing what's going on far better than I could. Please, be with Your servant Miriam now. Protect and comfort her.

It seemed she'd barely finished the prayer when she spotted the revolving lights on Ted's patrol car. The paramedic unit was on scene, too, and she grabbed her bag and rushed toward it, thanking God that the EMTs had gotten here so quickly. Miriam could use help from all of them.

The black buggy, smashed almost beyond recognition, lay on its side in the ditch, its battery-operated rear lantern still blinking. The big new sedan that had hit it, in comparison, looked barely touched, and she swallowed back anger at the unfairness of it all.

Ted met her at the rear of the unit. He grabbed her and swung her up next to the stretcher. "Let me have your keys," he murmured. "I'll see to your car."

She nodded, handing them over.

"Here's Fiona, Miriam. Just like you asked." The heartiness of his voice didn't quite mask his concern.

"Hi, Miriam." She kept her voice calm, even as her mind raced, considering possibilities. "How do you feel?"

Miriam's legs moved restlessly, and she turned her head from side to side, but she didn't speak.

Miriam lay on the stretcher, the paramedic opposite Fiona bending over her. Only one paramedic in the Suffolk Fire Department had those bright-red curls— her cousin, Terry.

"Terry. I'm glad it's you. How is she?"

Terry's blue eyes were dark with concern. "Bumps and bruises, mainly. Shaken and scared." She straightened, turning her head and lowering her voice. "She's holding her belly, terrified for the baby. We'd best take her in, I think. Maybe you'll have better luck than I have at reassuring her."

Nodding, Fiona edged past her in the narrow confines of the unit to take Terry's place at the side of the stretcher. She knelt, clasping Miriam's hand. The girl was pale, her blue eyes wide with shock, as she clung to Fiona's hand.

"Miriam, I'm here. We're going to take good care of you. We want to take you into the hospital. Is that okay?"

"If you say so," Miriam whispered. "My Jacob, is he all right?"

Fiona glanced toward Terry, who nodded as she closed the rear doors.

"He's fine," Terry said. "One of the officers is going to drive him to the hospital, while Fiona and I stay here with you."

Miriam nodded. She was pale, sweating, and her hand kept going to her abdomen. "My baby," she murmured, her voice fading as if she didn't want to ask the question.

Fiona looked up at Terry again. "Vitals?"

"Everything okay, but—" Terry shook her head. Obviously her instincts, like Fiona's, told her something more was wrong. "See if you can get her to talk to you."

Fiona held Miriam's hand between both of hers. "Miriam, you have to tell us what's wrong, so we can help you. It's all right. Honestly."

Tears spilled over on the girl's ashen cheeks. "Cramps," she whispered. "I kept having them today. I'm afraid for the baby. That's where we were going. I told Jacob he must take me to you."

Her heart clutched. Cramping happened sometimes early in pregnancy with no ill effect, but she didn't like it, not combined with the accident and the way Miriam acted.

"Okay, I'm just going to have a quick look. You hold on. We'll be at the hospital soon." She maneuvered to the foot of the stretcher as Terry slapped the door that led to the cab of the unit.

"Hit the siren, Jeff."

The van accelerated, swaying a little, as the siren started to wail. Fiona pushed Miriam's dark skirt aside, moving gently, and saw what she feared she'd see.

Her gaze met Terry's over the patient, and it was as if they could read each other's thoughts. The siren's wail was like a mournful cry, echoing the pain in her heart.

Ted stalked down the hospital corridor. Ironic. He'd ended up bringing the driver of the car to the same hospital where Miriam was being treated, but in his case it was for a blood alcohol test. A salesman, the driver had been out celebrating a big sale and decided to take a shortcut back to Suffolk. He must have been ripping along the dark country road. The buggy hadn't had a chance.

Ted would never be able to prove the speed, of course, with no witnesses, but the lack of skid marks told the story, and the results of the blood alcohol test would seal the case.

Unfortunately, that wasn't going to ease the pain Miriam and her husband were feeling.

He rounded a corner, hesitated, and then went forward. Miriam's and Jacob's parents waited, faces stoic, eyes bright with unshed tears. They must know what he'd just been told. Miriam had lost the baby.

"Joseph. Anna." Ted nodded toward the other set of parents, whom he didn't know as well as he did Jacob's family. "I'm very sorry."

"It is in God's hands," Joseph said. He clasped work-hardened hands together. His wife nodded, but Ted could feel her grief.

"Are you waiting to see Miriam?"

"The midwife is with her now." Joseph gestured slightly toward the door opposite them.

It stood ajar, and the tableau he saw made his breath catch. In the pool of light from a fixture above the bed, Fiona leaned forward, holding Miriam's hand, talking earnestly to her. Even in profile, he could see the warmth and caring that flowed from her toward the girl on the bed.

Jacob stood on the other side, head bent. Tears trickled into his beard, but he nodded, as if taking comfort from Fiona's words.

His throat tightened. Fiona had so much caring and devotion to give. This had to be tearing her up, too.

She moved, apparently catching sight of those who waited, and stood. She said something else, to the couple, and then bent to press her cheek against Miriam's before straightening and walking toward them.

She nodded to the parents, holding the door open so that they could file through. He heard Miriam give a soft cry at the sight of her mother, and the door swung shut, closing the family in, leaving him and Fiona alone in the hallway.

"Ted." Her voice trembled on the edge of tears. She wiped her eyes with her fingers. "I can't even begin to imagine—" She looked around blindly.

His heart twisted with pity. "Here." He grasped her arm and steered her toward a nearby door. "Let's go in the lounge."

Fortunately the room was empty. A lamp on the pale wood end table illuminated a hard-looking couch and a straight-backed chair. A few old magazines were strewn on a coffee table. He led her to the couch.

"Relax a minute. There's nothing else you can do for her now."

She sank down, covering her face with her hands. "There was nothing I could do at all. Terry and I were right there, but we couldn't save the pregnancy."

Anger burned along his veins. "The accident—"

"The accident didn't cause the miscarriage." She looked up at him and shoved her hair back with her fingers. Her eyes were red, but she seemed under control. "It would be unlikely, since the baby's so well protected at this early stage. Miriam told me she was already having cramping. Jacob was bringing her to see me when the car hit them."

Her lips trembled, and she pressed them tightly together.

He sat down next to her. "I wish it could have had a happier outcome for them. And for you." That was as close as he could come to comforting her.

"I don't matter," she said quickly. "But Miriam— well, I tried to reassure her. The obstetrician from the birthing center will check her out as well, but I don't see any reason why she shouldn't have a successful pregnancy the next time."

"That's good news."

She nodded, but anger flickered in her eyes. "I hope it doesn't make things any easier for the driver. He can't be held responsible for the miscarriage, but he ought to spend time inside a cell for this."

"He'll be prosecuted, believe me." Almost without willing it, his hand had covered hers where it lay on the couch between them. "I have enough evidence, which is fortunate because Jacob and Miriam won't testify against him."

"Won't testify?" She turned a fiery gaze on him. "What do you mean?"

"Just that." He understood, but it didn't make his job any easier. "It's not the Amish way. They'll forgive, and they won't turn to the law. Even if they were actively being persecuted, they would leave rather than fight back. It's a matter of religious conviction with them."

The anger drained away from her expression, leaving her pale and tired looking. "I guess maybe I need to work a little harder on the forgiveness aspect of being a Christian. Right now I can only ask God why this happened."

His fingers curled around hers. "I don't think He minds a few honest questions. Or even a little honest anger. At least I hope not, or I'm in trouble."

"Is that part of why you left the Amish community?" She turned slightly toward him, and for the first time he felt as if the barriers between them had weakened.

"Among other things." He shook his head. "I can never leave entirely. It's a part of me, even though I can't live the life."

"You're doing a balancing act between two worlds." She said what he had often thought, and it moved and startled him that the understanding could come from someone he thought of as an outsider.

"That's it. Sometimes I feel as if I really am one of the 'world people.' And then I'll hear someone blaming the Amish for causing accidents by driving buggies on public roads—"

"That's ridiculous."

"Yes." He felt the conviction harden in him. "Driving under the influence caused tonight's accident, and justice will be done because that's the law, not because I know and care about the folks who were injured."

"You can't stop caring." Her hand turned so that their palms touched, their fingers entwining, and her warmth flowed through that touch.

"No, I can't." He barely murmured the words.

Something—her closeness, the silent room, the touch of her hand—was making him loosen the grip he kept on his emotions. His gaze met hers, and he felt as if he were drowning in the cool gray depths of her eyes. "Fiona—"

It was no good. Nothing rational would come out of his mouth. Instead, all he wanted to do was follow his instinct. And instinct meant touching the curve of her smooth cheek, tilting her face toward his, covering her lips with his.

For an instant she seemed to hold back. And then she leaned into the embrace, her hand moving on his arm in a gentle caress. Tenderness flooded through him, and for a dizzying moment he thought he'd be content to stay this way for hours.

Unfortunately, reason clamored to be heard. This was a public room, and someone could walk in at any moment. He pressed his cheek against hers and then reluctantly drew back.

"I guess this isn't the right place," he murmured.

She looked dazed for an instant. Then she shook her head, as if needing to clear it, and managed to smile coolly, as if they hadn't just kissed each other senseless.

"I guess not." She rose, glancing around. "I must have left my bag in the ER. I'd better pick it up and head home."

He thought of touching her shoulder, but that probably wasn't a good idea, when it would just make him want to kiss her again. "You don't have your car here, remember? I had someone drive it back to your place. I'll drop you off."

There was a certain amount of wariness in the look she gave him, but she nodded. Well, he could understand that, because he felt the same. He needed to do some serious thinking before he let this relationship get any deeper.

But as he followed Fiona out into the hospital corridor, he knew he couldn't kid himself about one thing. He'd begun to care about her, maybe too much, and he couldn't do a thing about that.

Chapter Nine

Fiona stood in the afternoon sunshine on her porch, trying not to grin like an idiot as the latest of a flow of new patients climbed into the waiting black buggy. Five new patients in the past few days, and four of them were Amish.

Still smiling, she turned to look at the carved wooden sign beside her door: Fiona Flanagan, Nurse-Midwife. Was it her imagination, or did it glow a bit brighter today?

"Is something wrong with the sign?"

Ted's voice broke into her mood, but instead of shattering it, it just made her more optimistic. Cautious, but optimistic.

"Not at all. I was admiring it."

She turned to find him in that familiar posture, one foot planted on the step, his hand braced against the porch railing. He was in uniform, the light-gray shirt fitting snugly across his broad shoulders. The slant of sunlight brought out gold flecks in his brown hair. He looked good—good enough that she had to suppress the urge to put her arms around him.

She hadn't seen him for several days—not since that kiss at the hospital, in fact.

His gaze was focused on the sign, not on her. Did that imply that the memory made him uneasy or that he wanted to forget what had happened between them?

"It's not a bad piece of work, though I sound prideful when I say it."

"I take it 'prideful' is a no-no in the Amish world."

"You take it correctly." He smiled suddenly, the movement rearranging the hard planes of his face into something more approachable. "Although if polishing a buggy until it shines or stitching the most perfect quilt doesn't involve a tiny bit of pride, I'll eat my hat."

The smile nearly undid her, setting up ripples of warmth that had nothing to do with the sunshine. "I guess saying the words out loud is the problem." She flicked a bit of dust from the carved letters. "Actually, I was thinking that maybe the sign isn't so much a hope as a reality, the way things are going."

"New clients?" He leaned against the railing, apparently in no hurry to move on.

She couldn't suppress the grin. "Five of them, and four are Amish." She spread her hands wide. "I don't understand it. Really, I don't. And it's not just the new clients. In the past couple of days, people have suddenly started greeting me on the street as if I've been here for years. It's great, but a little unnerving."

She was looking to Ted for answers, she realized. Somehow she'd started depending on him for an interpretation of all the things she didn't understand in this new life of hers. Usually that realization would be a signal to run in the opposite direction, but she didn't feel like running.

His eyebrows lifted. "You honestly don't get it? It's because of Miriam."

"Miriam? But why? I didn't even succeed in saving her pregnancy."

Sorrow touched her, and the knowledge that no one could have done better didn't remove the sadness, although maybe it made it a little easier to bear.

He studied her face. "You've been out to the farm, I hear. How is she doing?"

"Physically, she's recovering nicely. Emotionally—" She could hear the frustration in her own voice. "I've tried to counsel her as I would any patient who's suffered a miscarriage."

"Is that a problem?"

She shrugged. "She's been reluctant to talk. I think her feelings are at war with accepting God's will. If she doesn't want to talk to me, that's fine, but she should talk to someone."

"Her sister's going to stay with her for a while. Maybe that will help." He smiled. "I know that was your suggestion. You aren't angry that Aaron told me that, are you? I mean with patient-doctor privilege and all…"

"I guess not." An answering smile tugged at her lips. "How do you know everything that happens?"

"Gossip," he said. "It's invaluable to a cop. I just wish it would turn up those vandals for me. So you shouldn't wonder about your five new patients. Everyone knows how kind you were."

"I only did what any midwife would do."

"Maybe so, but it was you. You were there for her. You went out of your way to stay with her and comfort her. People admire that."

Some emotion crossed his stolid face, but it was gone again so quickly that she wasn't sure what it was. Do you admire that, Ted?

"Even so—" she began, but he stopped the words by touching her hand. For a moment she couldn't think clearly enough to say anything.

"Let people appreciate you." The normally low timbre of his voice went even deeper. "Don't turn away from that, Fiona."

Was he talking about the inhabitants of Crossroads? Or about himself? If she had the courage to ask him that, what would he say?

"Ted Rittenhouse, are you just going to stand there like a moonstruck calf or are you going to hitch my horse?" a female voice complained behind them.

Fiona spun around, heat rushing to her cheeks. Her cousin Rachel leaned forward on the buggy seat, reins in her hands, blue eyes sparkling. Neither of them had even heard the buggy approach.

Rachel looked from Fiona to Ted with a satisfied smile, as if she enjoyed knowing she'd startled them.

Ted straightened, unhurried. "Since you ask so nicely, Miss Rachel, I'd be happy to give you a hand." He wrapped the line Rachel tossed him around the porch railing. The horse dropped its head and began munching the narrow strip of grass next to the steps.

"Rachel, it's nice to see you." And unexpected. She hadn't seen anything of her young cousin in days. "Can you come in?"

"I can stay only for a minute. I am on an errand." Rachel hopped down lightly from the high seat, ignoring the hand Ted held out to her. She came up the steps to Fiona, excitement dancing in her pert face.

Ted patted the mare's neck. "Just how fast were you coming down the road, young lady? Bessie's all sweated up."

Rachel made a face at him. "Not nearly so fast as the cars do."

For an instant Fiona saw the mangled buggy again, and heard Miriam's sobs. A shiver she couldn't control went through her. "You should be careful out on the road."

"I can be nothing but careful, with pokey old Bessie between the shafts." She caught Fiona's hand. "You will never guess why I have come."

"If she won't guess, Rachel, you'd best come right out and tell her," Ted said. "It's not polite to tease."

Rachel's fingers tightened on hers. "Our grandfather has asked me to come to see you. You are invited to supper on Saturday evening. The whole family will be there. You'll come, won't you?"

She couldn't respond. An invitation to supper with her mother's family was the last thing she'd expected after weeks of being ignored.

"You will come, won't you?" Rachel repeated, worry darkening her blue eyes. "I said for sure you would come if we asked you. Please, Cousin Fiona."

How could she resist Rachel's enthusiasm? "Of course I'll come. I appreciate the invitation."

And even if she never saw them again after this one night, at least she'd have had a glimpse of what her mother had come from. Maybe that would ease the restlessness within her.

Rachel let out her breath in a whoosh of relief. "That is good. And Ted is invited, too, so there will be someone else you know." She gave Ted a teasing glance. "You won't mind that, will you?"

Fiona paced across the waiting room Saturday evening, glancing out the bow windows for a glimpse of Ted. Were the dark skirt and blazer she wore suitable for supper with her mother's conservative Amish kin? She hadn't any idea.

Up to this point, when she'd gone into an Amish home, it had been in her professional capacity, and she hadn't thought much of what she wore. This evening was different.

She could have asked Ted's advice about what to

wear, but she'd been too embarrassed after that episode with Rachel—especially the girl's obvious enjoyment at teasing her and Ted about their friendship. Friendship, not relationship—she wouldn't admit to anything serious. Not yet.

Did the entire township recognize the attraction they held for each other? If so, she could just imagine the talk. She folded her arms across her chest, hugging herself.

The familiar response welled up in her. Walk away. Pretend it didn't happen. Pretend you don't care. That way no one can hurt you.

But the old way of reacting wasn't working for her any longer. She actually felt like taking a risk—on Ted, on her mother's family—even knowing she could get hurt. Maybe God had led her to a situation where she had to change and where the reward for change might be greater than she'd ever dared to hope.

She glanced at her watch. Ted had said he'd pick her up, but no cars were in sight, only one Amish buggy coming down the road. It pulled to a stop in front of her steps. Ted held the reins.

This was the last thing she'd expected, and it took a moment to recognize the feeling in the pit of her stomach as apprehension. Grabbing her handbag, she went quickly out the door and down the steps.

Ted jumped down as she approached. Wearing dark pants and a light-blue shirt, he looked as if he'd dressed to blend in, if not to match. She straightened her jacket.

Was she only imagining it, or did his blue eyes soften when he looked at her?

"I hope you don't mind." He gestured toward the buggy. "I borrowed this from my brother. I thought you might enjoy seeing how your relatives travel."

She tried to block out the image of the overturned buggy. "That's nice of you."

"Sorry." He apparently understood what she didn't say. "That was stupid of me. After the accident—well, it will just take a few minutes to go back and get the car."

He started to turn, and she stopped him with a quick touch on the arm. At least, she intended it to be quick, but somehow her hand lingered at the sensation of warmth and strength under the smooth cotton of the shirtsleeve.

"Don't. It's all right." She pulled her hand away, confused by the rush of feelings. "You're right. I would like to experience riding in a buggy." She glanced up at the step. "Rachel hops up and down so handily that I didn't realize it was that high. In this skirt—"

"Not to worry." He grasped her waist, the movement taking her breath away. "I'll help you." He lifted her easily.

She grasped the edge of the seat and pulled herself into place, hoping he couldn't see the flush she was sure colored her cheeks. "Thank you."

He paused for a moment, hand braced against the buggy, looking up at her. "Are you sure this is okay?"

"Positive." She managed a smile. "I want to understand how my mother lived. I think it will help me make sense of who I am."

He nodded, then walked quickly around the back of the vehicle and swung himself up easily. He picked up the reins with a sureness that reminded her that this had been part of his life, too, for a long time.

Could he ever leave that fully behind? Not living here, certainly. She'd think, having made the decision, that he'd want to be as far as possible from reminders of what he'd given up. Or had he come back out of lingering feelings for Emma? He hadn't given her any sense of that when she'd seen them together.

He clucked to the horse, and they moved off. The swaying of the high seat sent her off balance. She grasped the seat with one hand and pulled her skirt down with the other.

"Don't worry," Ted said. "You're dressed fine."

"Really?" She was ashamed of her need for reassurance. "I don't want to offend anyone."

"You won't. They're used to being around the English."

The English. The outsider. Well, she knew that role. She could cope. But what was Ted thinking about this invitation?

She glanced at him. The setting sun brought out glints of gold in his hair, gilding his tanned skin. The ease with which his body moved to accommodate the shifts of the buggy, the strength of his hands, holding the reins—she felt her attraction for him growing with each—well, maybe she'd better get the conversation moving.

"Are you okay with this? I mean, you've tried so

hard to protect my grandparents from being hurt by my presence."

He shrugged, frowning at the horse's back. "Maybe I was wrong to interfere. In any event, they've taken it out of my hands now."

It wasn't exactly a rousing vote of confidence, but it would have to do. "Have you heard anything about why they've changed their attitude?"

"I've always heard something, you know that." He smiled. "Apparently Emma and Rachel have been encouraging your grandmother to see you."

A frisson of apprehension slid down her spine. "I don't want to cause problems for her. What if seeing me brings back all her grief for her daughter?"

Ted grasped her hand firmly. "Don't overanalyze it, Fiona. She's asked for you. I don't see how you can do anything else but go."

The warmth from his hand traveled up her arm. "I guess I'm feeling protective of her, too."

He grinned. "There's a lot of that going around."

"You should know. I've never met anyone with a stronger protective sense." She swayed with the movement of the buggy, beginning to sense the rhythm of it.

"That's the police motto. To serve and protect." His tone was light, but there was a thread of something darker underneath it.

"People appreciate that," she said, wondering if appreciate was the right word.

His shoulders moved. "I guess. Amish folks might

not exactly approve of my profession, but at least they trust me. And I know I can trust them."

Emotion colored the words; they reached out and clutched her heart. This was important to him, maybe the most important thing.

"Is that why you came back to Crossroads? Because you could trust the people here?"

His eyes darkened, and for a moment she thought he'd tell her to mind her own business. Then he shrugged. "Maybe. Maybe I just realized I didn't belong in a big-city police force and never would."

"You were pretty young when you went there, weren't you?" She was feeling her way, trying to get at the source of all that suppressed emotion.

"Young. And naive." He gave a short laugh, but it didn't sound as if he found anything very humorous. "Talk about hayseed—I'm surprised I didn't literally have hay in my hair."

"That must have made it tough for you at the police academy." She tried to picture that young Amish farm boy thrown in with a bunch of tough cops. She couldn't quite reconcile that boy with the man he was now.

"I was the butt of every joke, believe me. I grew up in a hurry. I had to." He shrugged. "Things got better after a while. I still felt like a fish out of water, but I made some friends. It helped that I was doing what I really wanted to do." He glanced at her. "You know what that's like. If you're doing the work you know you're created to do, that makes up for a lot."

"Yes." Her voice choked a little. How was it that he seemed to see things in her that other people didn't, like the pain of trying to fit in? Maybe because he'd been through it, too. "So you started work as a Chicago cop."

"Saw things I'd never seen before, that's for sure." His jaw tightened. "Things I'd rather not see. Still, I had a good partner, an older cop who showed me the ropes. I'd have been lost without Steve."

"But something went wrong." She just seemed to know, the way he knew things about her. They turned into a lane, and she grasped the seat railing as she swayed against him. "What was it?"

The sun dipped below the horizon, painting the clouds with red and purple, as if it wanted to linger a bit longer.

"Went wrong. That's a nice way of putting it." His hands must have tightened on the reins, because the horse tossed its head. "We were in on a drug bust, a big one. Guess I was proud of my role in that. It seemed as if I was finally getting where I wanted to be."

He was silent for a moment, seeming to study the stubble of corn in the fields on either side of the road. She didn't speak, knowing there was more but afraid to push.

Finally he sighed. "Some of the drugs went missing. The investigation showed there weren't many people who'd had access to them. Internal Affairs got an anonymous tip that I was the one."

"But you—they couldn't accuse you on the basis of an anonymous tip."

"They didn't accuse me, exactly. I was suspended, pending investigation. It never occurred to me that anyone I knew could think I'd do something like that. I found out I was wrong. Everyone believed it. Even my partner." He paused. "Especially my partner." Bitterness laced the words.

"He was the one?" She barely breathed the words, her heart hurting for the pain and betrayal he'd suffered.

He nodded. "The truth came out, eventually. He was arrested. I was cleared. But it was never the same after that."

"The others must have tried to make things right with you."

"They did." He shrugged. "I couldn't blame them, I guess. But they hadn't trusted me, and I'd found out that I couldn't trust them."

"So you came home."

"I learned that trust was the one thing I couldn't live without. So I came home."

"As hard as it was," Fiona said softly. "It brought you back here, where you belong."

He didn't react for a moment, long enough for her to wish she'd said something else. Then he actually chuckled, putting his arm around her shoulders and drawing her closer against him. She could feel the laugh moving in his midsection.

"I never thought I'd say this, but you remind me of my brother Jacob."

She pictured the Amish carpenter. "I do?"

"The one and only time we talked about what happened to me in Chicago, he said pretty much the same thing. He said it reminded him of the story of Joseph."

She blinked. "You mean Joseph in the Old Testament? I guess he did have some grief over not being trusted."

"True, but that's not what my brother was thinking about. He reminded me that even when he was betrayed by those he'd loved, Joseph could still forgive. And he could say that even though they'd meant what they did for evil, God meant it for good." He snuggled her closer to his side. "I didn't see it that way at first, but I've come to think Jacob was right."

She nodded, thinking of her own favorite verse. "I try to believe that 'in all things, God works for the good of those who love Him.' Sometimes it's not easy."

"I know. But once I accepted that, I realized I was exactly where I was meant to be." He smiled. "Even if God did have to hit me upside the head with a two by four to get me here."

She thought about the implication of his words, warmed both by the strength of his body next to her and by his confiding in her. Their bodies swayed together with the movement of the buggy, and she wished the ride could go on forever.

It couldn't, of course. They were almost to the farmhouse, and she had to find a way through the difficult times ahead. Maybe, thanks to Ted, she was a little more ready to face them.

Chapter Ten

Ted drew into a spot in the lineup of buggies near the barn and slid down. It looked as if the whole Stolzfus extended family had already arrived and was waiting for them.

Maybe it would have been better if he'd brought the car. Somehow the buggy had a way of encouraging intimate conversation. That was the only explanation he could think of for having told Fiona all of that. He didn't normally talk about what had happened to him—hadn't, in fact, since he'd unburdened himself to his brother when he'd first come back to Crossroads.

He took his time fastening the horse to the hitching rail and walking around the buggy, trying to get a handle on this need to confide in someone he'd only known a month. After all, he'd known he could trust Jacob to tell people only what they needed to hear. Did he really trust Fiona that way?

Trust was a precious thing. He'd grown up taking it

for granted, not knowing how valuable it was until he'd lost it. He'd have to guess that confiding in her said something about the feelings he was starting to have for Fiona.

He reached up to help her down from the high buggy seat. Her face was tight with apprehension, so he squeezed her hand. She had enough on her plate right now without adding him and his concerns to the mix.

Besides, the habit of caution was strong within him. He wouldn't do or say anything he might have cause to regret.

He held her hand a moment longer than he had to. "Are you ready to do this?"

She nodded, trying to smile and not quite succeeding. "You will give me a kick under the table if I make any bloopers, won't you?"

"You've got it." The impulse to continue holding her hand was strong, but he beat it back. "Don't worry. You'll be fine. And you already know Emma and Rachel. They'll help."

They walked together toward the kitchen door. Did she realize that in the country, family and friends always came and went by the back door? He'd given it some thought, but he wasn't going to lead Fiona to the front door, as if she were a stranger. She belonged, whether anyone wanted to admit it or not.

They'd barely reached the steps when the door was thrown open and Rachel was smiling at them. "You're here at last. And you came by buggy."

"I thought Fiona would enjoy it." He stood back to let Fiona enter first.

She hesitated for an instant before moving, but Rachel grabbed her hands and drew her inside.

"Ach, your hands are cold." Rachel frowned at him. "Ted, you should have warned her she might need mittens."

"Yes, ma'am, I should have. You'd make a good boss, Rachel, you know that?"

"Better than some I know." She put her arm around Fiona's waist. "Now you must meet the family. Don't worry about remembering everyone's name."

Ted ducked his head slightly, coming into the kitchen. The doorway hadn't been made for someone his height. Since he was behind Fiona, he got the full effect of all those pairs of eyes focused on her. It was intimidating enough, and that was just the few who were in the kitchen. Goodness knew how many Stolzfus kin would eventually gather around for the meal.

To her credit, Fiona didn't freeze. She moved forward, greeting Emma with what might have been relief in her voice at the sight of a familiar face. He stood back, letting Emma take over introducing Fiona to the other women.

Her grandmother, he noticed, wasn't yet present. Was she still over in the daadi haus, the cottage the older couple had retired to when eldest son Daniel had taken over the farm? Was she perhaps regretting this visit?

If Fiona wondered about her grandmother's absence, it didn't show, as she politely greeted one woman after another. The elder Stolzfus couple had had five children—Hannah the eldest, Emma the youngest, and the three boys sandwiched in between, but the family had grown with marriages and children and those children's marriages until they'd probably sit down close to thirty around the long tables.

He'd known them all his life, and he had a tad of difficulty keeping all the young ones straight, but Fiona seemed to be doing a fine job of it. Because it meant so much to her, or because she was determined not to appear rude in front of all these unfamiliar family members? He wasn't sure.

The men, hearing all the fuss, began filing in to be introduced. He was just exchanging a few words about the winter wheat with Daniel when a silence fell over the crowded kitchen. John Stolzfus stood in the doorway, his tall frame bent a little with age, his beard snowy white below his weathered face.

For a moment he and Fiona stared at each other. Then he nodded gravely. "You are welcome in our house, Fiona."

"I'm pleased to be here," she answered, just as formally. "It was kind of you to invite me."

He turned toward Mary, Daniel's wife, with a question about supper. That seemed to break the tension, and a hum of conversation began again. Ted edged forward as unobtrusively as possible until he stood beside Fiona.

"So far, so good," he murmured.

She glanced at him. "Is it good?" He heard the fear in her voice.

"Plain folks are always a little formal with newcomers." That wasn't really an explanation, and he knew it. "Just give this a little time. It'll work out."

"I wish—"

Whatever she wished, he apparently wasn't going to hear it, as Mary directed everyone to the table except for her appointed helpers.

"In other words, she wants all non-essential personnel out of the kitchen." He touched Fiona's arm, nudging her toward the two long tables that had been set up to accommodate the crowd. "I hope you brought your appetite, because someone's sure to be disappointed if you don't try everything."

"Ach, don't listen to him," Emma said, whisking past them to deposit a steaming bowl of potatoes on the table. "Just be sure you have my cucumbers in sour cream. And don't forget to eat yourself full." Smiling, she scurried back toward the kitchen for another load.

He was holding out a chair for Fiona when he felt her fingers tighten on his arm. He looked up.

Her grandmother came toward the table, moving slowly. It wasn't until she reached the chair next to her husband that she glanced toward those gathering around the table. It felt to him as if each person held his or her breath.

Louise placed one hand on the table, leaning on it as she seemed to force herself to look at Fiona. The silence stretched. Even the children were still. Louise's lips trembled, her eyes filling with tears. Then she nodded and sat down heavily.

Fiona's fingers dug into his arm, and the tension zigzagged from her to him and back again. He sensed the battle going on inside her. Gently, he nudged her toward the chair.

She sat down, and he settled into the seat next to her. If all he could do to help her was be beside her, that was what he'd do.

The meal had begun with a long prayer in German and continued through a bewildering assortment of dishes to an array of pies and cakes for dessert. When Emma had said she should eat herself full, she hadn't been kidding. Fiona felt as if she'd split a seam in her jacket if she ate another bite.

Chicken, ham, chicken pot pie, pickled beets, hot potato salad, molded salads…the food seemed endless. Some of the dishes she'd never tasted before, like the dried corn casserole, with its nutty flavor, and the relish her aunt called chow-chow, made, she said, with everything that was left in the garden at the end of the season. Obviously the Amish didn't like to let anything go to waste.

Fiona glanced at Ted, who had three different kinds of pie on his plate and was eating through them happily. The slice of dried apple pie she'd taken was delicious, but she couldn't possibly finish it.

Emma leaned over her chair and took the plate. "I will make you a basket to take home for tomorrow," she said.

Ted looked up at her. "What about me? Don't I get a basket?"

"You already had more than your share, you did." She cuffed him on the shoulder, gave him a sisterly smile and carried plates toward the kitchen.

Her grandfather's chair scraped as he stood, and he said something in the low German that was the home language for the Amish. Ted leaned closer to translate, his warm breath stirring her hair.

"The kids are scattering to do their chores, and the men will wander out of range of any dishwashing. It might be a good move if you offered to help in the kitchen." He looked at her rather tentatively, as if afraid she'd consider that comment a putdown.

"Of course I'll help." She slid her chair back. "You go smoke a pipe, or whatever the guy thing is."

He nodded and followed Fiona's uncles toward the front porch. She picked up a couple of serving bowls. In spite of her confident words, she still felt unsure of her welcome.

Ted paused at the door, glancing back, and gave her a smile and a thumbs-up sign. When she turned, her answering smile lingering on her lips, she found Emma watching the doorway where Ted had disappeared, her face unreadable.

Did Emma resent what she saw when she looked at the two of them? If Rachel was aware of their attraction, surely Emma would be, too. She might be remembering her first love, and how it had ended because of Fiona's mother.

Emma turned, saw Fiona watching her and smiled, eyes twinkling. "That Ted, he is a good boy, ja?"

"Not a boy any longer."

"No, I forget." Emma put her arm companionably around Fiona's waist as they walked to the kitchen. "To me he is always the boy he was."

"The boy you loved?" She couldn't believe she'd actually said the words.

"We were sweethearts, ja, once upon a time. But our paths went different ways, and I have never regretted my choice." She handed Fiona a dish towel, seeming to take it for granted that she would help. "I would be very happy if you and he found yourselves on the same path."

"We're—we're just friends," she said quickly, taking the hot bowl Mary had just set in the dish drainer. "That's all." She rubbed the bowl vigorously, hoping her expression didn't give anything away.

Emma scraped plates into a bucket that sat next to the sink. "That's too bad, that is. It's time for Ted to settle down, don't you think?"

The question seemed to be addressed to the whole room, and a chorus of agreement answered her question. Cheeks burning, Fiona picked up another bowl.

"We won't tease you anymore," Sarah said. Daniel and Mary's eldest daughter was a slightly more mature version of Rachel, with her rosy cheeks and blond hair, but with round glasses that gave her a more serious air. "You and your coming-to-call friend want to take your time, ja?"

It was probably useless to say that Ted wasn't her coming-to-call friend, and she'd welcome anything that would get them off the subject. "Yes, that's right," she said, mentally apologizing to Ted for the evasion.

Sarah's intervention seemed to work, because the conversation steered away from her, bouncing around the kitchen from woman to woman in time with the clink of dishes. She sorted them out, finally, in the little breathing space it gave her.

Mary, Daniel's wife, was clearly in charge, a cheerful, buxom woman who seemed to relish her role as farmer's wife and who directed the household in a calm, firm manner. Was she what Hannah would have been, if she'd stayed?

There was Sarah, her eldest daughter, who taught in the Amish school, followed by a couple of boys, then Rachel, then young Levi, the baby of the family. The boys had headed for the barn to do evening chores, but the girls hung around, helping in the kitchen, joining in the cheerful conversation.

The wives of her mother's other two brothers were there, too—shy, quiet Anna and hearty Margaret, whose laugh bubbled like a flowing brook. Their daughters, hair in braids, were younger than Rachel, who seemed to enjoy bossing them around as they helped.

Would this have been her life if her father had sent her back to Hannah's family instead of putting her in foster care? Would she have been sweet and sassy, like Rachel, or would she have rebelled, like her mother?

She couldn't change the past, but she couldn't help wondering. She'd never want to give up her career, but still, she envied them this family warmth and the secure place they had in their world.

"Your practice, it goes well, does it?" Anna reached across her to put silverware in a drawer.

"It has been picking up. I've had a few long drives this week to some outlying farms."

"Ach, yes, you had best hope Margaret Beachey does not go into labor on a rainy night. Your automobile could get lost in the mud puddles in their lane."

"If she took the old road over the ridge—" Sarah began.

"She would never find it in the dark," Margaret said. "Better she tells Amos Beachey to fix his lane if he wants the midwife to make it to his wife in time."

Apparently Amos Beachey was known for being the only Amishman in the valley who didn't keep his farm in good order, so that led to one silly suggestion after another about how to solve the problem.

The only one who didn't join in the lively talk was her grandmother. Fiona glanced at her quickly, not wanting to be caught staring. Her grandmother seemed to be taking a very long time putting leftovers in the gas-powered refrigerator. Maybe she welcomed that as an excuse not to talk.

And maybe all the lively conversation the others provided was a screen to mask her grandmother's silence. Or a way of protecting her from the pain caused by Fiona's presence.

I don't want to hurt her. I just don't know what to do. Please—

The kitchen fell silent as abruptly as if someone had turned a switch. Her grandmother walked toward her. Fiona held her breath, not sure what was happening. Her grandmother reached out, almost tentatively, and touched her cheek.

"At first I thought there was nothing in you of my Hannah," she said slowly. "But I look into your eyes, and I see her there."

Fiona's throat went tight. "I never knew where my gray eyes came from, until I came here."

"It was right that you came." Her grandmother's cheeks glistened with tears, but she smiled. "When I first saw the quilt, I was afraid, but that was wrong."

"I'm sorry," she said quickly. "About bringing the quilt pieces to Ruth's that day. I didn't realize anyone would recognize them."

"It makes no matter." Her grandmother patted her cheek. "The quilt is a good thing. Emma will finish piecing it soon."

That brought a gasp from Emma. "You know about it?"

"Ja, I know. And when the quilt top is ready, we will have a quilting party. Fiona will come, and we will all finish her mother's quilt together. That is what is right."

She could only stand there like an idiot, trying to keep the tears from spilling over, her heart ready to burst.

* * *

The clop-clop of the horse's hooves echoed on the dark ribbon of road as Ted turned the buggy back toward Crossroads. Fiona hugged her jacket closer around her against the evening chill, but the cold air didn't really bother her. She was still warmed by her grandmother's hug when she'd said goodbye to everyone at the farm.

"Cold?" Ted reached behind the seat with his free hand and pulled out a plaid blanket, spreading it over her lap. "Is that better?"

"I'm fine." The happiness that bubbled up within her wanted to burst free. "I can't tell you what this evening meant to me."

She glanced back, watching as the yellow lights of the house disappeared behind a row of trees. She could see the reflection of the red battery-powered lantern as it blinked a soft good-night from the back of the buggy.

Ted's arm slid comfortably around her shoulders. "I'm glad it worked out. I take it your grandmother finally talked to you."

"She did. She said I reminded her of my mother. No one ever said that to me before." Her throat got tight at the thought. "I guess I didn't realize how much I wanted to hear that."

"Hannah would be happy that her daughter and her mother are together."

That didn't seem to need an answer, and she just let the thought settle into her heart. Her mother would be happy. That was a good way of thinking about it, making her feel the strength of family connection, threading from mother to daughter through the generations.

Ted drew her a little closer, and she rested her head against his shoulder, enjoying the solid strength of him. Despite the chill, the night was perfect, with a nearly full moon riding low over the nearest ridge. The only sound was the clop of the horse's hooves, the creak of the buggy's wheels and the rustle of grass along the road as some night creature passed.

"Look," Ted said softly.

The buggy's lantern cast its yellow circle on a red fox that stood at the edge of the road, head high, nostrils quivering as it deciphered their scent. Then it was gone in a blur of scarlet, darting off into the shelter of the stubbly field.

"Beautiful." She tilted her head to look up into his face. "That's not something I'd ever see in San Francisco."

"I guess not. Do you miss it? The city, I mean."

"Not a bit." The realization startled her. "I thought I'd find it lonely here, but instead I feel as if I've come home."

"That's good." His face was so close to hers that she felt his breath, stirring the hair at her temple. "You've found family here, to make up for the ones you left behind."

He didn't understand about her family. He couldn't, because she'd never talked to him about it. Now the silence, the darkness, the sense that the two of them were alone in the world all combined to suggest she could tell him anything.

She paused for a heartbeat or two. "I've been wondering what my life would have been like if my father had sent me back here after my mother died, instead of putting me into foster care."

"Foster care?" He drew back a little, searching her face in the dim light. "He didn't keep you?"

"He couldn't." Odd, to be defensive about her father's actions after all this time. "I mean, there he was alone in a strange city, his wife dead, no family to help him. It was the only thing he could do."

Even in the dim light, she could see his jaw tighten. "Sweetheart, I can think of plenty of other things he might have done—day care, a nanny, sent you back here, either to his family or Hannah's. Seems to me any of those things would have been better than giving you to strangers."

Sweetheart. The word echoed in her heart.

"I can't argue about that, because that's what I've been thinking, too. I did go back to live with him, eventually. After he remarried, when my stepmother was pregnant and decided to leave her job, then they took me home with them."

"Big of them."

The suppressed anger in Ted's voice caught her by surprise.

"I guess they did the best they could," she said carefully. Trying to be fair; she always tried to be fair. "It can't have been easy, adjusting to a six-year-old who'd been

raised by other people. Once their children came along—
well, they were a complete family without me."

"And you were on the outside, looking in."

Again she sensed his anger and was comforted that
it was on her behalf. She looked up, finding his face only
a breath away from hers, and for an instant lost track of
what she was going to say.

"It's all right. It doesn't matter to me the way it used
to." She thought about the scripture passage he'd mentioned earlier. "Maybe, in a way I haven't yet seen, God
means it for good."

"You have family now. People to care about you."
His voice went to a low rumble on the words. "That's
good, isn't it?"

Yes, she did have that. Somehow she didn't want to
confess to him that she was still wary of all those people
who seemed to want to care about her, a little afraid of
how she felt about them. That was cowardly, wasn't it?

"Fiona?" He touched her cheek gently, caressingly.

Her heart was beating so loudly that surely he could
hear it. "Don't—don't you have to hang on to the reins
with one hand, at least?"

"Nope." He smoothed her hair back, the touch of his
fingers sending waves of awareness through her. "Sophie
could take us home if I didn't touch the reins at all."

He was going to kiss her. That was what she
wanted, wasn't it? So why did she feel as if she
trembled on the edge of a precipice, ready to topple
over in an instant?

Then his lips found hers, and she stopped thinking at all. Only feeling—feeling the tenderness of his kiss, the strength of his arms around her, the steady beat of his heart under her hand as she turned into his arms. There was a precipice, and she was falling, head over heels. Falling in love with him.

Chapter Eleven

He was going to see Fiona on business. Wasn't he? Ted walked past Ruth's store, aware of an urge to quicken his steps as he drew closer.

Sure he was. Never mind that he'd have found some excuse to seek her out anyway, after last night.

He hadn't been able to dismiss the memory of that kiss. That alone should have been enough to set the cautious habits of years on high alert. He hadn't felt this way since—well, maybe since the thrill of his first love.

Caution was probably a good idea. He and Fiona were very different, and she was struggling with who she was and where she belonged. Still, she wouldn't have kissed him the way she had unless she was interested.

So, he was combining business with pleasure. He had to talk to Fiona again about his continuing search for the vandals. He frowned. They'd struck again, probably at about the time he was taking the slow route back to Fiona's in the buggy.

The front of Fiona's house came into view. She'd planted bronze and yellow mums in pots along the porch recently. Every time he saw the place she seemed more settled. The sign he'd made for her looked good—as if it were where it belonged, too.

A buggy was drawn up to the front of the house. Well, what did he think—that she'd be sitting there waiting for him to come along? Naturally she'd be busy, with her practice increasing the way it was.

Aaron Yoder leaned against the buggy. The young man might have looked relaxed, but Ted detected the nervous strain in his shoulders and the way he rubbed his hand up and down his pant leg.

"Aaron." He braced one hand against the buggy. "Your Susie in seeing the midwife?"

Aaron nodded, swallowing. "Susie thinks it will be time soon."

"That's good news. I'm sure she's tired of waiting."

"Ja." He managed a smile. "Tired. She rearranges the clothes for the little one a dozen times a day. She's had me move the cradle every five minutes, it seems."

"It'll be over soon." He clapped Aaron's shoulder. "Then she'll be too busy with the baby to think of anything else."

Even as he spoke, the door opened. Susie emerged, looking so pregnant it was a wonder she could move. Aaron sprang toward her to help her down the steps, glancing up at Fiona, who'd come onto the porch after Susie.

"It will be soon, ja?"

She smiled, her hand on Susie's back. "Soon, but not today. Probably not tomorrow, either, but you can never be sure. Babies arrive when they want to, not when we want them to."

Susie smoothed her hand over her belly. "This one isn't listening to me, that's for sure, or he or she would already be here."

"Come back in a week, if nothing has happened by then. Or send Aaron for me, anytime."

The expression on Fiona's face when she watched the pregnant woman was something to see. It wasn't just the devotion to her patient—Ted had seen that before. This was a sense of pure pleasure, as if anticipating the birth gave her as much joy as it gave the parents.

He helped Aaron maneuver his very pregnant wife up to the buggy seat. "Take good care of her, Aaron."

"I will that." Aaron tucked a blanket across Susie's knees, then clucked to the mare, and they moved slowly off.

Ted turned toward Fiona. "You look as happy as if she were related to you."

"Do I?" The smile lingered on her face. "I guess I do feel that way about all of my moms. It's such a joy, especially when everything's going well and the parents are so eager. But even when it's a difficult situation, there's still that pure joy of helping new life into the world."

Each time he saw her, he found more things to admire about this woman. "I don't know much about midwives, but I'd say you must be one of the best."

She smiled, shaking her head. "The people who trained me set a high standard. Some of them were true pioneers in having midwifery accepted by the medical establishment." She turned toward the house. "Will you come in?"

"I think I'd better." He followed her up the steps.

She turned a questioning look on him. "Is this a professional call, then?"

"In part." He held the door open for her. "I'd have come anyway, to tell you how much I appreciated being with you last night."

Her cheeks flooded with color as rosy as the top she wore. "And I appreciated your support, more than I can say." She gestured toward the door to her office. "Come in here. I don't expect any other patients this afternoon."

He glanced around as he entered, taking his time, taking it all in. His brother's bookcases were filled with books now, except for the ones closest to Fiona's desk, which carried neat stacks of pamphlets on childbirth. The graceful windows that were the first thing he'd noticed about the house were filled now with potted geraniums on one side and African violets on the other.

"Nice, very nice." Everything from the flowers to the braided rug on the polished floor to the comfortable padded visitor's chairs to the small fountain that gurgled on a side table seemed designed to set a nervous client at ease. It was a far cry from his utilitarian police station. "You've made this very welcoming."

"My Flanagan aunt and cousins helped." She sat down—not behind the desk, but in one of the pair of chairs, gesturing him to the other one. "Tell me what's going on. Is this about the vandals?"

He nodded. "They hit again last night, probably about the time we were on our way home."

If the reminder of that ride home had embarrassed her a few minutes earlier, she was probably determined not to show it again. "What happened?" Apprehension darkened her eyes. "I hope it wasn't too bad."

"It could have been, but luckily they were heard." He frowned absently at the twined strands of the braided rug. With a bit of luck, he hoped this business with the vandals would arrange itself as neatly. "They drove a vehicle through the fence out at Mose Stetler's place— you remember him, the Amish carpenter?"

"Of course. What happened?"

"I guess everyone's nerves have been on edge lately. Mose heard them and went running out. They'd ripped through what was left of the vegetable garden and were headed toward the barn." His jaw clenched. He could almost see the scene as Mose had described it. "Before he could reach them, they'd smashed a burning lantern into the hay he had stacked in the shed next to the barn."

Fiona's hands clasped, as if in prayer. "Is he all right? Did the barn catch fire?"

"He got there in time to beat it out. A couple of

minutes later and he might have been too late." He thumped his palm on the chair's arm. "They're escalating. I've got to catch them before they hurt someone."

"I know." She leaned toward him, her face distressed. "I wish I could help more, but I've already told you everything I saw."

"One thing—maybe they're getting a little overconfident. They didn't bother with the dark sweatshirts this time. Mose caught a glimpse of a local high school jacket."

She drew in a breath, something startled and aware in her face.

"Fiona, what is it?" He swung toward her so that their knees were almost touching. "What did you remember?"

"Not anything from the night Ruth's store was vandalized." She was shaking her head, as if to push a memory away. "It's nothing. It must have been a coincidence."

He clasped her hand firmly in his. "Tell me what it is. Let me decide if it's a coincidence."

"At the auction." Her gaze was troubled. "I think I might have mentioned it to you. There were four boys—they went running by, jostling me, on purpose, I thought. Three wore high school jackets, and the fourth was Amish."

The moment she'd said the words, Fiona regretted it. She could see by Ted's expression that he thought this meant something, but how could it? There were probably hundreds of teenage boys in the township, and running around was what kids did best.

"Did you recognize any of them?" That was his crisp cop's voice.

She shook her head. "I didn't know many people in town then. I certainly didn't know them."

"What about now? Picture them in your mind. Have you seen any of them since?"

She pulled her hand away from his, clasping them both in her lap. "It was just a glimpse. If I did see them now, I probably wouldn't recognize them."

"You're not trying." He leaned toward her, face intent. "Picture it happening again. What did you see?"

She closed her eyes briefly, hoping that would convince him that she was trying. "Blue jeans, high-school jackets. Those pricey sneakers all the kids seem to wear. I didn't really get a look at anyone's face—they went by too quickly."

"What about the Amish kid?"

Frustration gripped her. "I just saw him from the back. He looked like any Amish boy—dark clothes, fair hair under a black hat. It could have been anyone."

He leaned back in the chair, and she didn't care for the way he was studying her. "Maybe if you took a walk around the high school, you'd spot one of them."

"I couldn't possibly identify anyone. And even if somebody did look familiar, you can't arrest him on that." He wasn't leaning toward her any longer, but she still had the sense that he was pressuring her.

"I wouldn't be relying on that for an arrest, but it might give me a lead. At the moment, I have nothing."

"You haven't told anyone that I reported the vandals in Ruth's store, have you? You said you'd keep it quiet. But if I went wandering around the high school, it wouldn't take people long to figure it out."

"You have a point." He frowned. "That would certainly alert them. I want to catch them, not just scare them off. Look, what about glancing through the school yearbook?"

"How could I possibly pick anyone out that way?" She wanted to shake him until he accepted that. "Even if I did, there's not a shred of evidence that the boys at the auction are the vandals."

"Maybe not, but it's odd, three high school boys ramming around the auction in the company of an Amish kid. That doesn't often happen."

"I still can't—"

"What's really going on here, Fiona?" Ted planted both hands on the arms of the chair. "You're stonewalling everything I suggest. I agree, this might be a wild-goose chase, but I have to do something. Don't you want to help?"

Her throat went tight. She hated arguing with him, hated feeling that she was letting him down, and she had a feeling he wasn't going to understand her reasons.

"Look, it's not that I don't want to help. It's just that I'm finally starting to feel as if I belong here. You of all people know how difficult it's been."

He tried to interrupt, but she swept on, riding a wave of determination not to lose what she'd found.

"If the Amish were practically ready to boycott me

because I'm Hannah's daughter, what do you think they'll do if I turn in one of their kids for vandalism? And what about the rest of the community? They'd go right back to seeing me as an outsider, interfering in their business." Maybe that was selfish, but she risked losing everything she'd built here.

His jaw looked as hard as iron. "You can't let that keep you from doing your duty."

"It's not my duty. Maybe it's yours, but it's not mine." Why couldn't he see that she only wanted to live in peace?

He shoved himself out of the chair and stood for a moment, towering over her. Just looking at her. Finally he shook his head.

"I know how much you want to belong here. But if you're going to accept the advantages of belonging, I'd think you'd be willing to accept the responsibilities, too. I guess you're not."

He turned and walked out. She didn't call him back.

Fiona hung up the phone and walked slowly toward the hall, touching the lush blossoms of the geraniums on the windowsill as she passed them. Her office had turned out well, but now she couldn't think of that without remembering Ted admiring it. Somehow all of her thoughts of this place were tangled up with him.

And now with the disappointment he'd shown yesterday when she'd refused to help him.

Not refused, she corrected quickly. She couldn't help him. Didn't he understand that?

She knew perfectly well why she'd made that call to San Francisco. She'd needed to talk to her friend, to someone from that other life, who'd understand why she'd reacted the way she had to Ted's suggestion.

Tracy had been supportive, and while Fiona was talking to her she'd felt perfectly justified. Unfortunately, once she'd hung up, all those rationalizations sounded hollow. Was she really refusing to take on the responsibility she should for her new community?

Frustrated with herself, and more than frustrated with Ted, she grabbed her handbag, making sure she had her cell phone, and went out the door, locking it behind her. She'd walk over to Ruth's store and have a chat. Maybe that would reassure her that she was doing the right thing, not risking what she had here.

The bell over the door jingled, seeming louder than normal, as she went inside the store. She glanced up at it, then at Ruth, who was coming toward her from the counter with a welcoming smile.

"Did you get a new bell?"

Ruth glanced at it, mouth quirking. "Sign of the times. Ted said I should be sure I could hear when someone came into the store." She shook her head. "I can remember when folks would come in, get what they wanted and leave the money on the counter. Now it's bells and alarm systems and not even trusting your neighbor."

"I'm sorry." Here was a different aspect—not a

question of law but one of being able to trust. "Did you put in an alarm system after the vandals hit your store?"

Ruth nodded, smoothing her hair back under her cap. "Ja, I decided Ted was right about that. I was fortunate that it wasn't worse—maybe something scared them off before they could do too much damage. Or somebody." She gave Fiona a bright-eyed, questioning look.

Fiona struggled to hold a polite, interested expression. There'd probably be no harm in letting Ruth know she'd called the police, but how would she know how fast that would spread, or how other people would react?

"I'm glad you have protection now. That must make you feel safer."

"That's true, but still I'm sorry for the need of it." She sighed. "Used to be I knew every living soul in Crossroads Township. Now, with all the new folks coming in from goodness knows where, with goodness knows what kind of values—" She stopped, flushing slightly, and reached for Fiona's hand. "I didn't mean you, no. After all, you're one of us."

Fiona wanted to hold on to that sense of belonging without adding in that little smidgen of guilt that Ted had induced. It would be nice if she could get his voice, and his disappointment, out of her mind.

"Goodness, I'm forgetting myself. Your aunt is in the workroom. You're probably here to see her, not listen to me babble."

"It's always a pleasure to see Emma, but yes, I actually came to see how you're doing." Somehow she hadn't been able to form the habit of saying 'Aunt Emma,' probably because Emma seemed like a contemporary of hers, instead of her mother's.

She went through the archway, minding her step on the old wooden floor that sloped erratically between the two sections of the store. When she got past the display rack, Emma was already looking up, smiling, obviously having heard her voice.

"It is good that you are here today. I was hoping to show you this." With a flick of her wrist, she unfurled the quilt top over the counter.

Fiona let out an audible gasp as she approached, reaching out to touch the flowing colors. The rose centers of each square drew her with their beauty, but the thing that truly caught her eye was the way Emma had put the patches together, so that the dark and light colors created diagonal stripes across the quilt.

"It's so beautiful." She touched one of the dark lines, realizing that it seemed to disappear as she looked closely at each patch, forming an optical illusion. "I love the effect."

"Will keep you warm at night," Emma said, her face showing the pride in her work that she wouldn't say aloud. "This design is called Log Cabin with Straight Furrows, like the furrows of a new-plowed field."

"Is it done?" She stroked the fabrics, longing to see it on her bed right now.

"Not yet." Emma's smile suggested that she knew what Fiona was thinking. "I must put the borders along the sides, and then it will be ready to add the batting and the backing, and we will quilt it together."

"I'm not much of a seamstress." She hated to think of ruining the beautiful thing with her crooked stitches.

"It makes no matter," Emma said. "We will all help you. When we all work together on a quilt, it is…" she hesitated, as if searching for the right words. "It is like sewing love into the quilt. For you."

Her heart was too full to speak easily. "Thank you." Their hands met over the quilt her mother had begun for her. "It means a great deal to me."

"To us, too." Emma patted her hand. "You are one of us, now."

One of us. The words echoed in her heart. Ted's voice seemed to provide the counterpoint. *You have to accept the responsibilities of belonging, too.*

Little though she wanted to admit it, he might have a point.

Chapter Twelve

Ted shoved the budget report away, frustrated. How could he concentrate on figures when his thoughts were totally wrapped up with people—people he cared about, people who were hurting. Or who would be hurting, if he didn't do something.

He ran his hand through his hair, then rubbed the back of his neck, feeling the tension that had gathered there since that early-morning phone call. If he ignored it—

Let justice roll down like the waters, and righteousness like an ever-rolling stream. If he didn't pursue justice, he was betraying everything he believed.

He had to do his job, even when he hated it. Like Fiona, who hated the idea of doing something that could get someone in trouble.

But Fiona was a civilian. She had the luxury of standing back, if that was what she chose to do. He didn't.

He'd probably been too harsh with her, but the

conflict that raged in her was too familiar for him to see clearly. He understood, too well, the cost of belonging. Maybe she was just beginning to find that out.

Getting up, he stretched, his hand bumping the wall. It reminded him of Fiona's comments the single time she'd been to his office. A shadow moved across the glass window in the office door. He looked, feeling the quickening of his pulse that he should have been getting used to by now. Apparently Fiona was about to pay her second visit.

She opened the door slowly. Her reluctance to enter was so strong he could feel it.

"Fiona. Come in."

She walked into the office, closing the door with far more care than it deserved. She apparently found looking at it preferable to looking at him.

He pulled the visitor's chair to a more welcoming angle. "What brings you to visit me?"

"I've been thinking." She cleared her throat. "About what you asked me to do. I still don't like it, but I've decided I should do as you asked and look at the high school yearbook."

"I see." The words came out slowly, but his mind was racing. What had changed her mind? It hadn't been anything he'd said—he'd messed up that conversation thoroughly. He gestured to the chair. "Please, have a seat."

She sat down, drawing her brown corduroy jacket around her. When she didn't speak, he knew he had to ask the question.

"What made you change your mind?"

She folded her hands in her lap, looking down at them. "Does it matter?"

He sat down on the corner of his desk, watching her. "Not to me as a cop, no. But to me as a friend—well, yes, it matters."

Her lips pressed tightly together. Maybe he'd made a mistake in pressing her. Or in referring to himself as a friend.

Finally she glanced up at him, her gray eyes troubled. "I've been thinking about what you said—about the responsibilities that come with belonging."

"And I've been thinking that maybe I crossed the line when I said that."

Her smile flickered. "Maybe. But perhaps I needed to hear it." She shrugged, the movement restless. "Since I came to Crossroads, I've begun to realize that I've been looking for a place to belong all my life. But I haven't thought about what that might cost."

"It's not easy." His mind touched on the perennial sore spot—the knowledge of the pain he'd caused his family by his choices.

"No, I guess it's not." She sat up very straight, as if to underscore her decision. "Do you have that yearbook for me to look through?"

He nodded, reaching across the desk to pick it up and hand it to her. "Take your time. You're not accusing anyone of anything, remember."

She didn't look convinced, but she took the book

with both hands. She began paging through it, scanning each page as carefully as if her happiness depended upon what she saw.

Watching her, he thought about the tidbit of new information that had come his way. He found himself wanting to share the burden with her, not only because she might help him rule it in or out, but because the load would be easier for him if he shared it.

But not easier for her, not by a long shot. The careful way she studied each page told him how conscientious she was, how concerned she was not to make a mistake.

The things she'd told him about her family life had shocked and saddened him. They'd also gone a long way toward explaining how guarded she was in some ways. She didn't want to risk the pain that could come from opening her heart.

She was just now beginning to take a step toward belonging. He didn't want to think about what it would do to her if that belonging were snatched away. If he asked her to help him further he was risking pain for her, to say nothing of endangering the fragile bond that had formed between them. Still, what choice did he have?

Her fingers touched a photo, and she drew in a deep breath and let it out. "I think this was one of the boys I saw at the auction." She shook her head. "Not just think. I'm sure."

"Okay." He moved to her side to look at the photo.

She glanced up at him. "I'm sorry, but I didn't realize until I saw the picture that I really could identify him.

I guess I got a better look than I thought when he rounded the corner."

He looked at the photo, his heart sinking. "Jared Michaels. He's just sixteen, but he's already had a couple of brushes with trouble."

"You know him?"

"I know everyone, remember? Somehow, I'm not surprised you picked out Jared's picture."

"I can only say that he was one of the boys at the auction. There's no connection between the auction and the vandals."

"Unfortunately, there is a link. Someone came back to the site of the auction that night and trashed the things that hadn't sold. Stuff was left sitting outside, so that made it easier for them."

"You didn't tell me that before." She frowned at him.

"If you hadn't been able to identify anyone, there'd have been no need for you to know."

He thought she might flare up at that, but she just nodded, her eyes thoughtful. "You don't look especially happy at having the boy identified," Fiona said. "What trouble has he been in?"

"Nothing serious. And unfortunately nothing he was ever held responsible for. His mother claimed her son couldn't possibly have done anything wrong, and his father took a 'boys will be boys' attitude."

"You think they'll do the same with this?"

"I think I'd like to have a little proof before I actually tackle Jared."

"Well, I wish you success with it." She stood up, obviously ready to escape.

He held out his hand to stop her. "There's something else."

"I didn't see enough of the other boys to be able—"

"It's not that." He took a breath. This was going to hurt her, but he didn't see any way out of it. "I received an anonymous tip this morning, saying the caller knew who the Amish boy was who's running with the vandals."

Her eyes darkened, as if she were bracing herself for bad news.

"Who?"

"Rachel's brother. Levi Stolzfus."

"I just can't believe it." Fiona took the curtain rod from her Aunt Siobhan's hand and mounted the step stool to slip one end into its bracket.

"Can't believe Levi would do it, or can't believe anyone would say that about him?"

Siobhan held the other end of the rod, her hand keeping the drape from dragging on the floor of Fiona's living room. Not only had her aunt insisted she had the perfect drapes for the room, she'd even hemmed them to fit and then come to help Fiona hang them.

"Both, I guess." She stepped back down, moved the stool and climbed up to take care of the other side. "He's such a quiet boy—I haven't gotten to know him as well as I have Rachel. But even so, I just can't believe it of him."

Did she really know him well enough to say? That was the question that had haunted her since she'd stormed out of Ted's office.

"What is he, about thirteen?" Her aunt smoothed the folds of the drapes. "That's a difficult age. Boys can become secretive and very easily influenced by their peers."

"You sound as if you speak from experience."

Siobhan smiled. "After the crew I raised? You can believe I speak from experience. What one of them didn't think of to do, the others did. And Ryan was the worst of the lot, always trying to outdo his older brothers with one outrageous trick after another."

"Well, now he's settled down to be a model husband and father, hasn't he?"

"That he has." Siobhan's face softened into a sweet smile. "I have to say that grandchildren are a wonderful reward for having raised your children."

"I'm sure they are." Although she couldn't imagine her stepmother thinking it a good thing for anyone to call her "Grandma."

She stepped down from her perch, stroking the floral print fabric with pleasure. "These really are beautiful. The colors are almost like a watercolor painting. You're sure you didn't need them any longer?"

"My husband said that he'd get hay fever if he had to sleep in a room that looked like a flower garden any longer."

"So you let him have his way."

She waved a hand in the air. "It was a pleasure. And now you can enjoy them."

Her aunt smiled as if she really enjoyed giving something up to make her husband happy. Well, maybe that went along with the fact that Siobhan and Joe were as obviously in love as any newlyweds.

"I *will* enjoy them." Fiona carried the step stool to the next window. "To say nothing of appreciating your hard work in fixing them."

Curtains for her living room from one aunt; a quilt for her bed from another. She wasn't used to the sensation of having all these relatives wanting to help her.

"What did your friend think about the likelihood of young Levi being involved?"

Ted. Her friend. She wasn't sure that was how she would describe their relationship at this point.

"I don't think he liked it much, but of course he has to investigate. It's his job." That came out rather tartly, and her aunt seemed to notice.

"Yes, it *is* his job. He certainly couldn't show favoritism toward someone just because he knows them."

"I know that." She went back up on the step stool and took the second rod her aunt handed her. "But it is his job, not mine."

Aunt Siobhan raised her eyebrows. "Has someone suggested that it's yours?"

She fitted the rod end carefully in place. "He keeps talking about the responsibility that comes with belonging, as if I should—"

She stopped. She really hadn't intended to say that much to anyone, although of course Aunt Siobhan was perfectly trustworthy.

"He wants you to do something." Siobhan took her hand as she clambered down. "And you don't want to."

"No. I don't." She may as well tell her aunt the rest of it. Surely Siobhan would agree with her. "He doesn't want to talk to Levi in any official way if he can help it. Not yet."

Her aunt nodded. "I can understand why he'd feel that way, given his friendship with the family."

"He wants *me* to do it." The words burst out of her. "Just because Rachel and Levi sometimes come to visit me, he thinks I can get him to admit it if he's involved."

"Is that how he put it? Try to get him to admit something?" Siobhan sounded doubtful.

"Well, not exactly." She was ashamed of herself for trying to make Ted's request sound worse that it was. "He just wants me to bring up the subject and see if Levi reacts. He seems to feel that if he is involved, he might be longing for someone to give him an opening to talk about it."

She looked at her aunt. The curtain fabric cascaded from her hands, making her look as if she held a bouquet of flowers.

"I don't want to be the one. Is that cowardly?"

"No one would think that." Siobhan's gaze was as loving as if she were counseling one of her own children. "But that's not really the point, is it? You don't want to feel as if you're betraying your family, just when you're starting to be accepted by them."

Everyone seemed to see that clearly. "That's not wrong, is it?"

"No, not wrong. But you know, if the boy is involved in these tricks, the sooner it ends, the better it will be for him. I can't imagine, from what you've said, that he's anything but a pawn for these older boys."

"If it's him." She still wasn't ready to concede that.

"If it's him," her aunt agreed. "Still, if it is, it would do him more harm not to stop him. What if they did something that hurt a person, instead of property? He could be held accountable, even if all he did was keep watch."

That sinking feeling was the recognition that she didn't have any choice in the matter. "So you think I should do this."

Siobhan stroked her shoulder gently. "I think you should pray about it and open your heart for God's answer. You'll know what to do when the time comes, I promise."

You'll know what to do when the time comes.

Aunt Siobhan's words sounded in Fiona's heart as she cleaned up after her last appointment the next day. Though they probably wouldn't recognize it, her aunt Siobhan and her aunt Emma were similar in many ways, especially in the fact that they were both strong women of God.

I want to be like them, Lord, but I don't feel very strong right now. Please guide me. Help me to find the answer.

She dropped a load of sheets into the washer in the

kitchen and started it, finding its hum companionable in the quiet house. Even with patients, family and new friends, the house still sometimes felt lonely.

The clop of a horse's hooves alerted her, and she looked out the kitchen window to see Rachel halting her buggy next to the back steps. She wasn't alone. Levi sat beside her.

Panic gripped her. *Not now, Lord. I'm not ready yet.* She'd asked God to help her find the answer, and He'd immediately presented her with an opportunity to do just that, ready or not.

She dried her hands and reached the door just as her young cousins did. Rachel beamed at her. "We surprise you, ja?"

"Yes, you do. Come in, please."

"I must do some shopping at Ruth's for my mother." She gave Levi a little push toward Fiona. "Levi does not like shopping. Is all right if he watches the television?"

She could hardly imagine this was anything but God's answer to her prayer, with the opportunity to talk to Levi alone thrust at her.

"Of course." She touched Levi's shoulder lightly. "Go on in, Levi. I'll fix a snack for you."

He nodded, not speaking, and headed down the hall. She glanced at Rachel, who was frowning at the doorway through which her brother had gone.

"Is anything wrong?"

"N-no." Rachel didn't sound as confident as she usually did. "It's just that Levi has been quiet—more quiet than usual. Often I can worm it out if something bothers him, but not this time." She shook her head. "I will come back soon. Thank you, Cousin Fiona."

She stood for a few minutes after Rachel left, hands braced against the counter. *Please, Lord.*

She took a breath. She knew what she had to do. The question was, could she do it? Well, she had to try.

Quickly, she took out the peanut butter, bread and jelly. It might be easier to talk over a snack, assuming she could get the boy to talk at all.

She put the sandwiches on a tray, added two glasses of milk, and carried the tray through to the waiting room, where Levi sat cross-legged on the rug in front of the television, gaze rapt on the flickering images on the screen.

Sitting down next to him, she held out the tray.

"Ser gut." He gave her a shy smile that made him look about eight. He took a bite of the sandwich, returning his attention to the television.

She couldn't possibly force a bite down her dry throat. Instead, she drained half a glass of milk.

Some cowardly part of her told her to get up, make an excuse and scurry back to the kitchen until Rachel returned. Don't get involved. That's safer. You can't get hurt that way.

But it was too late for that. She was already involved, and no matter what happened, she had to try.

She glanced at the television, looking for something to start the conversation. The show was typical cartoon fare, with plucky teen heroes battling monsters.

"I've never seen this one before. Is it good?"

Levi shrugged. "Is all right. Not as good as video games."

Something tightened inside her. "I've never played one of those. Do you like them?"

"You have to learn to control them." He gestured with his hands, as if working an imaginary control. "I learned fast."

That was so close to bragging that it took her aback for an instant. Without noticing it, she'd become accustomed to the ingrained Amish modesty.

"You must have some English friends to teach you video games." Who are they, Levi? What trouble did they lead you into?

"I have some. There's nothing bad with that." His voice turned defensive. "You are English, and you are my cousin."

"That's true," she said slowly. *Do it.* "Unless those English friends want you to do something you know is wrong. Then it might be very bad."

Levi stared at her, blue eyes widening. Then he dropped the remains of his sandwich, scrambled to his feet and bolted for the door.

"Levi—"

But by the time she reached the door, he was gone.

She stood in the doorway for a moment, arguing with herself. He hadn't admitted anything, had he? There was nothing that she could really tell Ted—no evidence that Levi was involved with the vandals.

But she couldn't fool herself about this. Something had been very wrong about the way the boy reacted.

Her aunt Siobhan's words came back to her again. If Levi was involved, the best thing for him was to be caught quickly, before anything else happened. She couldn't hide her head in the sand. She had to call Ted.

She glared at the phone a few minutes later, frustrated. It was one thing to get her courage screwed up to do this, and another to be confronted with nothing but an automatic answering machine instead of Ted.

If she waited until later—but that was the coward's way out, and she couldn't take that any longer. The message tone sounded.

"Ted, it's Fiona. I just had a conversation with my cousin. I think we'd better talk as soon as possible."

There, it was done. Why was it that doing the right thing felt so much like being a traitor?

Chapter Thirteen

"Look, I'm really sorry I didn't get back to you last night."

Ted stood just inside Fiona's kitchen doorway, because she hadn't offered him a seat. Judging by how annoyed she looked with him, it was a wonder she'd even let him in the door.

"That's all right." She didn't sound as if it was all right, but at least she'd said the words. Fiona poured a mug of coffee and held it out to him.

"Thanks." The mug warmed his palms, but it didn't take away the chill in the atmosphere.

He couldn't be irritated in return, because he knew the strain on her face was his fault. By the time he'd finally retrieved his messages and heard Fiona's voice, he'd told himself it was too late to disturb her. And today had been completely jammed, so that it wasn't until late afternoon that he'd been able to get here.

If her pale face and heavy eyes were any indication, she probably spent the night worrying about her cousin. He longed to offer her sympathy and reassurance, but unfortunately that was in short supply right now.

"Sit down," she said abruptly, pulling out a seat at the kitchen table. "Please," she added, as if realizing how short that had been.

"Right." He sat down across the table from her.

"I'm sorry." She pushed the waves of thick hair back from her forehead. "I didn't get much sleep last night."

"No, neither did I."

Her eyes widened, as if she were startled and frightened. "Why? What happened?"

"You first." He gestured toward her. He was a cop in the middle of an investigation, and he'd best remember that. "What did Levi say?"

He thought she'd protest at that, but she just frowned down at the dark brew. "He didn't really *say* much. He let it slip that he's been hanging around with some English friends, and he was pretty defensive about it."

"He mention any names?" Tension knifed through him. If that boy was involved in what had happened last night, a lot of people were going to be hurting.

Fiona shook her head. "It was like talking to a clam. So then I said that having English friends wasn't a problem, unless they wanted him to do things he knew were wrong."

"What did he say?" His fingers tightened on the mug.

"Nothing." She refused to look at him. "He jumped up and ran out of the house."

Heaviness settled in his heart. "I guess that tells us what we need to know, then."

"Maybe not." Her head came up. "It could mean a lot of things other than his being involved with the vandals."

"I suppose it might, but that's not all there is to it. Not now."

Apprehension filled her eyes. "What is it? What happened?"

He frowned. "Look, some of what I'm going to tell you is public knowledge, or soon will be. Some of it is police business, but I'm telling you because you're in a position to help."

Was that all? He wasn't sure any longer.

"I understand." She clasped her hands together tightly. "Just tell me."

"They're getting careless. And dangerous. They set fire to a barn last night at Marvin Douglas's place. Like they tried to do at Mose's farm." The chill he'd felt when he heard the fire alarm went down his spine again. "That's the worst thing a farmer can face—a barn burning. Old Marv's dairy cows were inside the barn."

"Oh, no." Fiona's face had gone even whiter. "How bad was it?"

"Marv's seventy-five if he's a day. He got the cows out all right, but the barn's a total loss. And he had a heart attack watching it burn."

Fiona's breath caught, her hand going to her lips as if to hold back a cry. "Is he—"

"In the hospital, in coronary care. He's a tough old bird—says he's fine and wants to go home."

"Could he identify the boys?"

"He didn't get a close enough look, but the vehicle he spotted sounded enough like Jared's to give me cause to run over there. I caught Jared and two of his buddies coming home—with empty beer bottles in the car and an empty kerosene can in the trunk."

"Not Levi?"

"No. But if he had been with them, they'd have dropped him off first."

"You sound as if you want him to be guilty." She flared up, eyes blazing.

For a fraction of a second he wanted to lash back. How dare she attack him, when he was doing the work he'd sworn to do?

The reaction seeped away when he recognized the pain in her face. She was trying to protect her cousin, trying desperately to believe he wouldn't do this.

"I don't want any such thing," he said evenly. "And I think you know that."

She put her hand up, seeming surprised to find a tear trickling down her cheek. "I'm sorry. I know you care about Levi. I shouldn't have said that."

"I want to help him, too, but the only way to do that is to find the truth."

"What happened to the other boys? Are they saying anything?"

"Nothing helpful." He frowned. "They haven't been

charged yet. I'd like to produce a bit more hard evidence before I do that. Jared was pretty cocky, practically daring me to arrest him. Naturally his parents don't believe he'd do anything as serious as setting a fire."

She paled. "I understand how they feel. That's how I feel about Levi."

"Levi hasn't been in a string of malicious mischief incidents dating back three or four years. And he's not mouthing off to police officers."

"I take it you don't care much for Jared."

There was more truth to that than he wanted to admit. "He actually hinted around, as if he was trying to blackmail me."

"Blackmail you? That's ridiculous." She was quick to his defense, and it warmed him.

"Influence, maybe is a better term. He was careful not to admit anything, but he hinted that I'd be unhappy if I found that fourth vandal." Ted reached across the table to put his hand over Fiona's. "He implied that it was someone close to me. Like Levi."

The words echoed in the quiet room.

Fiona couldn't say anything for a long moment. She could only stare at Ted, her heart pounding in her ears. His fingers tightened over hers.

"Did you believe him?" Ted knew Levi far better than she did. If he thought Levi capable of—no, she just couldn't buy that. "Ted, you can't believe Levi would set fire to a barn knowing there were cows inside. Maybe some of the other things, but not that."

The stern planes of his face seemed to harden. "A week ago I'd have said it was impossible. But the evidence keeps piling up."

She shook her head helplessly. Unable to sit there any longer, she crossed to the counter, staring out the window at the setting sun.

She heard the scrape of Ted's chair as he rose, the heavy tread of his feet coming toward her. His hands came down on her shoulders, lightly, tenderly, and his grip sent strength into her.

"I wish I saw my way clear in this." His voice was husky. "I don't want you to get hurt, Fiona."

She gave in to the longing to lean back against him, feeling the thud of her heart, the protectiveness of his arms around her. He pressed his cheek against her temple, and his breath feathered across her skin.

"I don't want to get hurt either, but I think it may be too late for that. I just hate to think how my grandparents will feel—"

"You can't tell them." He turned her to face him, and he was back to being the in-control cop again. "Not now. Not until I know for sure what the truth is."

She swallowed the argument she was tempted to make. Of course he was right. There was little sense in alarming them. Perhaps Ted would find that Levi hadn't been involved. She needed that to cling to.

"I won't." She took a step back, and his hands fell from her shoulders. "But you told me. Why?"

"Only because you were already involved, and—"

He stopped, his frown deepening until it set deep furrows between his straight brows.

"What is it?"

"Something was said when the three boys were together. Something I wasn't meant to overhear."

"Are you going to tell me what it was, or do I have to guess?" At his expression, a chill went down her spine that had nothing to do with the temperature.

His blue eyes darkened when they rested on her. "You were mentioned. The others hushed him up pretty fast when they saw I was there, but I'm sure of it."

"Me? How would they even know me?" She didn't want to admit being frightened at the thought.

"I don't know what it means, but I don't like it. Maybe it was something about you being Levi's kin. Maybe they figured out that you spotted them that night at Ruth's store. I don't know, but I had to warn you."

"You can't think they'd try to do anything to me. That's ridiculous. What could they possibly gain?"

"Nothing, but I'd say rational thinking isn't exactly their strong suit." He clasped her hands in a quick, hard grip. "Look, it's probably nothing. Use some of those urban smarts of yours and take precautions—lock your doors, keep the outside lights burning."

She nodded, less concerned for herself than she was for Levi. And for Ted. "What are you going to do?"

"Investigate. Try to find out the truth." His face was somber. "I love that boy, too, you know. But if he broke the law, he has to be held responsible."

* * *

Fiona was double-checking the contents of her delivery bag when she hear a soft sound—so soft, she couldn't be sure what it was. She glanced toward the office window. Darkness pressed on it.

Time had slipped away while she'd sat in the office after Ted left. Praying. Thinking. Trying to see her way through this difficult situation.

Keep your doors locked and your outside lights on, Ted had told her, and she'd forgotten those precautions already. He'd been overreacting, surely. This was Crossroads, not the big city.

Still, her heart thumped as she walked softly out into the hallway and peered into the waiting room. No one was at the front door—she'd be able to see that, even without the porch light on. She went quickly to the switches and turned the porch light on, just to be sure. Nothing.

The sound came again, and this time she recognized it—someone was tapping at the back door. Well, the vandals would hardly knock on her door. She stepped into the kitchen and saw a dark figure outlined against the glass. Her heart jolted before she realized that it was a woman in Amish dress.

She went quickly across the kitchen to open the door.

"Fiona." It was her grandmother. "I must talk with you, ja."

"Come in."

She caught her grandmother's hands and drew her into the warm kitchen. Louise's hands were cold in spite of the black woolen cape that covered her, and as she came into the light, Fiona was shocked by her expression. Her face was drawn and pale, her gray eyes red-rimmed.

"Please, sit down." She hadn't yet found the right thing to call her grandmother. She couldn't say Louise—it seemed too presumptuous, but Grandmother was a title she didn't want to use until she was invited to do so. "You're welcome in my house."

"I cannot stay long." She took the chair Rachel usually sat in and pushed the cape back off her shoulders, revealing the now-familiar dark dress and apron. "I came because someone said that you were the one who saw."

"Saw what?" She sat down opposite her grandmother, tension tightening her nerves.

"The people who broke into Ruth's store." Louise's eyes were dark with apprehension, her face taut. "Emma heard that you were the one who saw that night. Who called the police. That is true?"

Apparently there was little point in trying to keep it secret now. Everything was out in the open, or would be soon. "Yes. I heard the intruders, and I called Ted."

"And you saw." Her grandmother reached across the table to grip Fiona's hand. Her fingers seemed worn to the bone but still strong. "You saw them."

"Not to identify," she said quickly. "Just shadows, running away in the dark."

"It is true?" Her voice held anguish. "One of the boys, the one who kept watch, he was Amish?"

Fiona's heart twisted. Everything she'd feared about this was coming to pass, and there was no way to avoid it. She nodded.

Her grandmother took a shaky breath, and her face tightened until it seemed the wrinkled skin was a roadmap of all the grief of her lifetime. "Was it Levi?"

Pain ricocheted through her. "I couldn't see, honestly. Only an outline of a boy in Amish clothing. It could have been anyone." She tried not to think about what Ted had said, about how the circle of suspicion seemed to be narrowing around her young cousin.

Her grandmother stared at her, gray eyes boring into her, as if searching past all evasions for the truth. "There is more, Fiona. I can see it in your face. Tell me what it is that you know."

Pain gripped her heart. Ted had ordered her not to tell, but she couldn't lie to her grandmother. Ted should know that. She couldn't pretend that she didn't know where the police investigation was headed and let the family find out in some other, more painful way.

"I'm sorry," she whispered. "I understand that one of the boys they've identified mentioned Levi's name. There's nothing certain, no one's come right out and accused him—"

But her grandmother's expression collapsed in grief. Tears welled in her eyes, and she put work-worn hands up to cover her face.

"Please, don't." Fiona sprang from her chair and rounded the table to put her arms around the bent figure.

"I'm so sorry. Nothing is certain—we don't know that he's done anything."

For just a moment her grandmother clung to her, arms tight around Fiona's waist. Then she pushed to her feet and wrapped herself in the black cloak.

"I must go." Louise turned toward the door.

"Grandmother—" The word was out without her thinking about it.

Her grandmother clutched her hand briefly. "It is in God's hands now."

She rushed out, leaving Fiona staring after her, her eyes wet with tears.

Chapter Fourteen

Saturday morning was usually Fiona's time to catch up with laundry and household chores, but she couldn't seem to settle to anything. Her mind kept returning again and again to the situation with Levi. What was happening with the family? What had her grandmother done when she'd run out the previous evening?

She couldn't keep Ted out of her thoughts, either. This was so difficult for him, too. He had such protective loyalty to his Amish roots, but an equally strong duty to his job. The conflict had to be tearing him apart.

She'd made a promise to him that she hadn't kept, agreeing that she wouldn't tell anyone about the accusation against Levi. She'd meant it when she'd agreed, and she didn't take breaking her word lightly.

But what else could she have done in the face of her grandmother's pain?

Bracing her hands against the washer lid, she stared blankly at the controls, unable to focus.

Lord, I don't know what to do, or even how to pray about it. Please, no matter what the truth is about Levi's involvement, work in this situation to bring good for him and his family.

She put her hands to her face, surprised to find it wet with tears. She dashed the tears away, straightening. She had been caught unwillingly in this situation, but she wouldn't let it control her. For all she knew, it might be days or even weeks until the investigation was concluded.

Switching on the washer, she turned and walked quickly through the house to the front door. With no clients to see, her day was her own unless Susie Yoder went into labor. She wouldn't spend it moping in the house. Grabbing her bag and jacket and checking to be sure she had her cell phone, she hurried outside.

The crisp autumn air had a bite to it, and the chrysanthemums glowed golden. It was a day that made one think of orange pumpkins, corn stalks and apple cider. Probably Ruth's store carried the apple cider, if not the pumpkins and corn stalks. She headed for the store, feeling better now that she had a destination.

As she approached the door she glimpsed, through the glass, an Amish couple standing with Ruth near the counter, heads together, deep in conversation. She opened the door, the bell jingling, and all three turned to look at her, faces as startled as if she'd been the subject of their conversation.

She was being paranoid, thinking such a thing. She pinned a smile to her face and advanced toward the counter.

The couple turned, faces grave, and nodded as they passed her. Ruth stared blankly for a moment before managing an unconvincing smile.

"Ruth, what's wrong?" Fiona felt as if a cold wind had swept through the store. "You look…" She wasn't sure how to finish that thought.

"You haven't heard?" Ruth's gray brows lifted. "It's all over the township. I thought surely you knew."

Her nerves prickled, but she tried to speak lightly. "I must be out of the loop. What's all over the township?"

"The police have charged four boys with the vandalism. Three English teenagers." Ruth blinked, looking away. "And Levi Stolzfus."

Telling herself she'd expected it didn't seem to do much good. Tears welled in her eyes, and she blinked them back. "No. I didn't know."

How could she? No one had come to her—not Ted, not someone from the family. That was a separate hurt in her pain over Levi.

Ruth looked at her, frowning a little. "But wasn't it you who saw them when they ran away from here? That's what everyone is saying."

"No. I mean, I had a glimpse of them running away from the store, but I didn't see enough to identify anyone."

"Why didn't you say anything to me then?" Ruth tipped her head to one side, considering. "Ach, I see. Ted told you to be still about it. Well, it's out in the open now. Poor Louise."

Her heart clenched at the mention of her grandmother. "Have you heard anything about how she's doing?"

"Not a word about any of the family. But surely they've been in touch with you."

"Not yet." It took an effort not to let pain show in her voice or her face. Maybe they wouldn't be in touch at all. The family would close in on themselves in a crisis, she already knew that. And she was on the outside.

She tried to swallow the lump in her throat. She could go to them, but their relationship was too new to test it in this way. And she knew in her heart she didn't have the courage to face the possibility that they would turn her away.

There was one other person who knew what was happening. She had to see Ted.

Fiona approached Ted's office door, her steps slowing. She could see him through the window, much as she'd seen Ruth and the Amish couple at the store.

Ted sat at his desk, perfectly still, frowning at something in front of him. His expression froze her hand on the knob. His face was taut with pain, maybe even grief. And it struck her that no one should be watching that private display of feelings.

No one, including her. Especially not her. No matter how close they'd drawn to each other in the past weeks, she didn't have the right. In the midst of her own pain over what had happened, she couldn't let herself forget that he was hurting, too.

And if he knew she'd told Louise what she'd promised not to tell, he'd be angry with her. Well, she'd just have to face that.

She took a breath, trying to still the pounding of her heart, and fumbled deliberately with the knob, giving him warning of her approach. By the time she had the door open and had stepped inside, his face had smoothed into its usual stolid expression.

"Fiona." There was no welcome in the way he said her name. He stood, as if good manners compelled that, but he didn't ask her to take the chair in front of his desk.

That steady stare made her nervous. "I…I'm sorry to interrupt. I wanted to find out about Levi, and I didn't know who else to ask."

For a long moment she didn't think he'd answer at all. Finally that rocky façade cracked just a little.

"All four of the boys have been charged and released into their parents' custody." His tone was cool and formal.

Relief washed over her. "He's home, then." At the back of her mind there'd been an image of her young cousin locked in a cell somewhere.

He gave a curt nod.

Thank You, Lord.

"What will happen next?" She took an impulsive step toward him, but stopped when he seemed to tighten in response.

"It's in the hands of the district attorney now. There

will be a hearing in juvenile court, although it's possible that Jared could be charged as an adult."

"But Levi—surely, if he was only a lookout…" She still found it impossible to believe that he'd willingly participated in destruction.

If it were possible for stone to harden, Ted's face did just that. "I can't discuss an ongoing case with you."

"An ongoing case? This is my cousin, not just any ordinary case."

"Not in the eyes of the law. I can't talk about it with you, Fiona."

A shaft of anger pierced her. "Why not? You weren't so reluctant to talk about the case when you wanted my help, were you?"

His fists braced against the desk so hard that the knuckles were white. "You were a witness. It was your duty to help in the investigation."

"I did help." Her voice wavered, and she fought to control it. "I helped, and now a member of my family is charged with a crime, and you won't even talk to me about it. I have a right to know—"

"I had a right to expect you to keep your promise, didn't I?" His eyes blazed with more emotion than she'd ever seen in him. "I trusted you with police information, and you broke that trust."

So, he knew about her grandmother's visit. Of course he'd see it that way. She'd been a fool to think he'd understand. "My grandmother came to me. She'd already heard rumors about me, about Levi. What else could I do?"

"You could have kept your word." A muscle in his jaw twitched, as if he tried to hold back and couldn't. "I went out to the farm expecting to have a private conversation with Levi and his parents. Instead, thanks to you, I had to face the whole church."

Her breath caught. "They didn't try to stop you—"

"They wouldn't do that." His eyes darkened. "They just watched while I arrested one of their own."

His pain reached out and clutched her heart. She could see the scene in his eyes—those dark, motionless figures, the faces of people he'd known and loved all his life, watching while he did what he knew was his duty, the act that sliced apart his roots and his calling.

Trust. He'd come back here after that horrible experience in Chicago, because here he could trust and be trusted. Now, as he saw it, she'd betrayed his trust. That was the one thing he'd never be able to forgive.

"You really don't have to help with this." Nolie took the stack of dishes from Fiona's hands. "You go back in and talk to Siobhan while I get the coffee and pie ready."

"No use." Siobhan came through the door from the dining room into the kitchen at Gabe and Nolie's farmhouse. "I'm here. Those men are talking fire department business again, and I don't have a thing to contribute to the conversation. I may as well help with the dishes."

Nolie laughed, setting the dishes in the sink that was ready with hot, soapy water. "That's all this family talks about, Fiona. You should know that by now. Unless we have the medical contingent together, that is. With you, me, Terry, her fiancé and Mary Kate, we ought to be able to outtalk the fire department once in a while."

"The rest of them aren't here," Siobhan said, measuring coffee into the coffeemaker. "You may as well be resigned to hearing firehouse talk."

Fiona busied herself with setting out the plates for the cherry pie her aunt Siobhan had brought, letting the other two women carry on with their laughing chatter. The invitation to dinner with Nolie and Gabe and her aunt and uncle had saved her from another lonely, depressing evening like the one she'd spent last night.

Yesterday Ted had cut away their promising relationship as if it meant nothing at all. As if the moments when he'd held her in his arms and kissed her hadn't existed.

And none of the Stolzfus family had come near her since Levi's arrest. It seemed they too had shut her out.

She surely had grounds for sorrow. Small wonder she welcomed cheerful company.

Unfortunately, the clatter of dishes and chatter of women's voices was too reminiscent of being in her grandmother's kitchen, feeling a part of her mother's family at last. Now that was an illusion.

At least she had her practice. So far none of her patients had left her, and she could only pray that continued.

She'd come here to establish her midwife practice, not to look for relationships. If she had that, she shouldn't ask for more. Besides, she still had the Flanagans.

Nolie went through into the dining room with a tray of cups and silver. Aunt Siobhan put her arm around Fiona's waist. "Are you all right, dear? You seem very quiet tonight."

She managed a smile. "Just enjoying the talk, even when it is about the fire department."

"I thought perhaps you were worried about that cousin of yours. Does he have a good attorney?"

So Siobhan knew about that. It had probably been in the Suffolk newspapers already. The arrest of an Amish teen made news. "The Amish don't believe in being entangled with the law. Ruth says they're not likely to hire a lawyer."

"The court will appoint someone then." Concern filled her aunt's face. "We know a fine young attorney—someone who's helped Brendan with some of his parishioners. Maybe we could get her to volunteer to take the case."

"Would you?" Tears stung Fiona's eyes at the unexpected offer of help. "I'd be happy to pay an attorney, but I don't want to seem to interfere."

"I'll talk to her." Siobhan looked at Fiona, a question in her eyes. "Has this created problems for you with Ted Rittenhouse? It seemed the two of you were getting fairly close."

"We're—we're just acquaintances, that's all." She

couldn't tell her aunt the truth about Ted without tears, so it was best if she said nothing.

Siobhan hugged her, as if she heard all the things Fiona didn't say.

Nolie came back in from the dining room, shaking her head. "You won't believe it. Gabe's radio went off with a fire call, and they're both hanging over it as if they're still on active duty."

"My husband's like an old fire horse," Siobhan said, crossing to the coffeemaker. "Ready to run the minute he hears the alarm. I suspect Gabe is just as bad."

They were still smiling at the image when Gabe appeared in the doorway, Uncle Joe right behind him. The expression on Gabe's face wiped away the smiles in an instant. He looked at Fiona.

She grasped the back of a kitchen chair, somehow knowing she needed its support. "What is it? What's happened?"

"It's a three-alarm from the Crossroads volunteers. Two companies from Suffolk are responding." He took a step toward her. "I'm sorry, Fiona. The building that's burning—it's your house."

She lost a few minutes then, probably from shock. She found herself being propelled toward Gabe's car by Siobhan and Nolie. Nolie gave her a fierce hug.

"I'm sorry I can't come, but someone has to stay with the baby. You're better off with Gabe."

"It's all right." Her aunt pushed her gently into the back seat. "Joe and I will be with you. It's going to be all right."

Was it? As soon as he and his father were settled in the front seat, Gabe took off, lights flashing from the top of the car and a siren wailing in the night.

"I guess it helps to have firefighter relatives at a time like this." She tried to say the words lightly, but her voice was choked with emotion.

This couldn't be happening. It couldn't. It must have been a mistake. *Please, God*— Somehow she couldn't even find the words to pray.

Aunt Siobhan clasped both her hands, holding them warmly. "Let's pray," she said softly, and Fiona nodded.

"Father, You know we're in trouble now." Siobhan's voice was as conversational as if she spoke to a dear friend. "We ask for Your help in this situation. Be with those who are fighting this fire. Grant them Your protection and surround them with Your love. We pray for the preservation of Fiona's practice. She's doing Your healing work in the world, Father. Please be with her and help her now. Amen."

"Amen," the men said together from the front seat.

"Amen," Fiona whispered.

Her aunt's first thoughts had been for the people who were in danger, fighting the fire. Shame filled her that she hadn't thought of them first, too.

Please, Lord, be with them. Ted would be among them—she knew that as if she were there watching. He'd be a part of the volunteer force. *Please, protect him.*

Chapter Fifteen

"Start wetting down the side and roof of the general store!" Ted shouted the orders to the crew of the tanker truck that had just pulled up at the fire scene. His personal feelings might tell him to direct every weapon toward saving Fiona's house, but as chief of the volunteer fire company, his duty was to the entire community.

His jaw tightened. He'd been telling the township supervisors for years that they needed a new tanker, but no one listened. He wanted to have them here this instant, to see how inadequate their small tanker was. Crossroads was lucky to have good neighboring companies to call on.

Thing was, he was angry at everyone and everything, especially the fire, for what this was going to do to Fiona.

The crew chief, head of one of the other small volunteer companies in the county, nodded. He gestured to his crew to drag the heavy hoses toward the general store. It was safe at the moment, but a brisk autumn breeze, blowing now toward the rear yards, could switch directions at any moment.

Townsfolk already swarmed into the store, carrying everything they could to safety, and the auxiliary was working just as quickly, setting up coffee and water in the sheltered area in front of the barbershop.

Mac Leonard, one of his volunteers, paused by the rig. Mac's breath was coming too fast. At nearly seventy, he shouldn't be on the fire line, but it was almost impossible to turn away volunteers.

"You want us to try and get anything else out?" Mac nodded toward the meager pile of furnishings they'd pulled out of Fiona's house.

Ted hardened his heart against the thought of Fiona's grief, knowing he couldn't risk lives for her beloved possessions. "No. It's spreading too fast. If those other units from Suffolk get here in time, maybe we can save something else."

Even as he said the words, he heard the welcome wail of the sirens. Suffolk's professional force provided training and much-needed support to the volunteer companies in the countryside.

The sight of the crews pouring off the hook-and-ladder and tanker he'd requested seemed to energize the volunteers, and a ragged cheer went up. He recognized the company commander headed his way—Seth Flanagan. He'd known Seth in a professional capacity for a couple of years, and now he knew him as Fiona's cousin.

Flanagan's face was tight as he watched smoke pouring from the windows of his cousin's house.

"Fiona wasn't home," Ted said quickly.

"I know. She's at my brother's. They're on their way now. Where's the water source?"

"Creek about fifty yards behind the house." He pointed. "Just follow our lines back."

Flanagan nodded and turned to his crew, giving rapid orders.

Fiona was on her way. His heart twisted. He couldn't kid himself. Seth Flanagan knew as well as he did that the structure was already too involved. All that dry old wood had gone up like so much tinder. They'd give it their best battle, but in the end, they weren't going to save the house.

The fire broke through the front wall, erupting upward as it met the wood of the porch. People gasped, stopping to watch, faces somber.

One of the men on the hose line stumbled, and Ted leaped forward to drag him away.

"Take a break," he urged. He grabbed the line himself until another volunteer came forward to take his place.

He'd barely turned away from the hose when a stir went through the crowd. A car pulled up, stopping just beyond the tanker. People spilled out the doors. In the eerie orange glow of the fire, he saw Fiona. Her mouth opened in a cry. She darted toward the building.

Heart pounding, he started to run toward her, but the people who were with her—her relatives, he realized—held her back, surrounding her with loving arms.

Foolish, that instinctive need he'd had to race to her. She had family to take care of her.

An ominous crack sent him spinning back to the fire. "Get back! Everyone back!"

His shout was drowned in the roar as the roof caved in. He did a quick count, making sure his people were safe. He couldn't bear to look at Fiona, but he felt her grief as surely as if he held her in his arms.

The next hour passed in a haze of activity, until finally they were wetting down the embers and he could take stock of the damage. Not good, but he guessed it could have been worse. No one had died. Fiona's house was a total loss, but there hadn't been any damage to the surrounding buildings except for a few broken windows and a layer of soot to be cleaned away.

Still, he didn't suppose Fiona was in any shape to hear that this could have been worse. Her work, her home, had been destroyed. He forced himself to look toward her.

At some time during the past hour, the Stolzfus family had arrived, too. Family from both sides clustered around Fiona, trying to comfort her. His throat, already raw from the smoke, tightened as he saw Fiona folded in the arms of her grandmother and grandfather Stolzfus.

In everything, God works for the good of those who love Him. It was tough to understand how God was bringing good out of this circumstance, but if a man didn't have faith, he didn't have anything.

Maybe it would cheer Fiona to know that they'd

saved a few things. He bent, picking up the wooden dower box he'd spotted on her dresser when he'd done a sweep of the house, and carried it over to where she stood. The cluster of family members parted, letting him approach.

"Fiona, I'm sorry." His voice rasped on the words. "I wish we could have saved the house for you."

She didn't seem to hear him. Her gaze was focused on the smoldering remains of her life, her eyes wide with what he knew was shock. Gabe Flanagan, the cousin he'd met at the farm, put his arm around her shoulders.

"Come on, Fiona. There's nothing you can do here. Let's go back to our place."

She shook her head, not moving. Gabe looked at him, helpless, clearly not sure what to do. He seemed to be expecting something from Ted.

Small help he could be, but he had to try. "We managed to pull a few things out before it got too bad."

Fiona still didn't react. He wasn't even sure she heard him.

"This was on your dresser." He shoved the box into her hands. "I thought it might be important."

Her hands grasped the box instinctively. She looked at it, and suddenly tears streamed down her face. Her body shook with sobs.

Aghast, he reached for the box, but her grandmother stopped him, shaking her head. "No. This is good. She needs to weep now."

All he could do was nod and turn away. Fiona didn't

need him—not now that she had the family she'd always wanted.

But as he looked at the smoking rubble, unexpected fury surged through him. The arson squad would be here in the morning, and he'd be right at their heels. He would know the truth about this fire, no matter what.

"Maybe you should go back to Crossroads today." Nolie sat down opposite Fiona at the sturdy pine kitchen table in the farmhouse, her face concerned. "It's been over a week. Wouldn't you at least like to see what things they were able to save from the fire?"

Fiona wrapped her fingers around the steaming mug of tea in front of her, trying to absorb some of its warmth. She stared past Nolie's worried face, out the kitchen window. As if to echo the devastation in her heart, the weather had turned colder, and frost had nipped all but the hardiest flowers in Nolie's garden.

"Not today. Maybe tomorrow I'll go."

It was the same thing she'd said every day for a week, and Nolie had accepted the words. But her expression grew more worried each day.

"So many people have been asking for you." Nolie coaxed her as if Fiona were her toddler daughter. "Don't you want to see them?"

Fiona's mind winced away from the thought. To see the people of Crossroads, to see the ruins of the life she'd tried to build there—no, she couldn't. She wasn't ready.

You're hiding, the voice of her conscience said. That's what you always do.

"I can't. Not yet. Not until I've decided what I'm going to do. The birthing center will handle my patients until then."

That was what kept her frozen, unable to move from the comfortable hiding place she'd found at Gabe and Nolie's farm. What would she do? What could she do?

"You'll rebuild, of course." Nolie sounded confident. "You own the land, and your insurance—"

She shook her head. "My insurance wasn't enough to cover all that I've lost, and I'd invested everything I had in the practice. In a year, I'd have been out of the red, but as it is—"

As it was, she felt crushed beneath a load of mortgage payments for a house and a business that weren't there any longer.

"Everyone wants to help." Nolie covered Fiona's hand with hers, and Fiona felt the warmth of her caring. "We'll find a way for you to rebuild. Just tell us what you want to do, and we'll help."

Her throat tightened. They were all so loving and helpful, these two families she'd so unexpectedly come to call her own. It wasn't fair to hold them hostage to her inability to make up her mind.

"I know. I'm sorry." Her throat tightened. "I guess I didn't realize how much that place had become home to me until it was gone." The furniture she'd picked out with such care, the cozy office, the living room Siobhan and Nolie had helped her paint—all of that was turned to ash. She tried to focus. "I know that's not an excuse to mope around, but I can't seem to get moving."

The telephone rang. With a sympathetic pat on her hand, Nolie went to answer it. In a moment, she turned back to Fiona, an odd expression on her face.

"It's for you," she said. "It's your father."

Fiona gingerly took the phone Nolie held out to her. Maybe Nolie had misunderstood who was calling. Her father hadn't spoken with her in over a month—not since he'd made clear what he thought of her foolish plan to relocate to Pennsylvania. It was as if, once she'd left California, he'd wiped her from his thoughts and his life.

"Hello. Dad?"

"How are you, Fiona?" Her father's voice was unexpectedly gentle. "I heard about the fire. Are you all right?"

"Fine." Well, she wasn't, but he wouldn't want to hear that. "How did you hear about it?"

"My brother called me." He cleared his throat. "Funny, to hear his voice after all these years. He sounds well."

"Yes." They could have talked to each other at any time in the past twenty-five years, if they weren't both so stubborn, but it wasn't her place to tell him that. "The whole family has been very helpful."

I've found a place here, Dad, that I never found with you. Why was that? She'd probably never know the answer to that.

"Well, I..." Surprisingly, her confident father sounded unsure of himself. "Your stepmother and I wanted you to know how sorry we are about your troubles. We want to help. Whether you want to rebuild or come back to California, you can count on us for financial support."

The offer was so unexpected that her throat closed for an instant. She hadn't asked, or been offered, any help since the moment she'd graduated from college. It had simply been understood that her father had discharged his obligation to her and that she was on her own.

"Thank you." She managed to get the words out, even though they sounded rather choked. "I—I haven't decided yet what I'm going to do, but I'll be in touch."

"Good." Her father's voice had that hearty tone it always took on at any display of emotion. "I'll talk to you soon, then. Goodbye."

She hung up, knowing the face she turned to Nolie must express her total bewilderment. "Uncle Joe called him. And he wants to help."

"Well, it's about time." Nolie's blue eyes shone suddenly with tears. "Siobhan must be so glad that they're talking again, even if it took a disaster to accomplish it."

Fiona nodded, feeling like smiling for the first time in a week. "At least something good came out of this."

Her own words startled her, and she blinked. Was she actually able to admit that God was bringing something good out of the grief that overwhelmed her?

The telephone rang again. Shaking her head, Nolie picked up. Her expression changed in an instant. "She'll be right there," she said.

"What is it?" If this was another effort to get her to Crossroads—

"That was Susie Yoder's neighbor. Susie's in labor. I guess it's time for you to saddle up and get back to delivering babies."

Fiona could only stare blankly at Nolie. "But I—I referred Susie to the birthing clinic in Suffolk. I thought she was going to go there."

"The neighbor says she's determined about this, and Aaron can't budge her. She's having her baby at home, and you're going to deliver it."

"I don't have anything. My delivery kit was in the house."

It was more than that, and she knew it. It was as if the fire had burned away her confidence when it burned her belongings.

"Well, then, I guess it's lucky that the staff from the birthing clinic dropped off a new delivery kit to replace the one you lost." Nolie tossed a jacket toward her and hustled her toward the door. "It's in your car, ready for you. Babies don't wait for anyone, not even the midwife."

Nolie's words seemed a catalyst, sending energy surging through her, chasing away the inertia that had held her paralyzed. Fiona grabbed her bag and cell phone and thrust her arms into the jacket sleeves.

"You know, you're right." She smiled, suddenly feeling like herself again. In this, at least, she knew what to do. "I guess the midwife had better get moving."

* * *

"You're definitely in labor."

Fiona's assurance seemed to take some of the tension from Susie's face. She leaned back in the rocking chair, reaching out to touch the hand-carved cradle that was a new piece of furniture in the simple bedroom since the last time Fiona had been to the house.

"Ja, *gut.*" The stress of the moment seemed to send Susie back to the Low German that was everyday speech for the Amish. "I thought yes, but I didn't want to call you out for nothing, slow as this baby has been to decide to come."

Fiona patted her shoulder. "That's fine. I'd rather be called out on twenty false alarms than miss the real thing."

The numbness that had gripped her since the night of the fire had vanished in the need to do the thing she was trained for—the thing she was meant to do.

"How soon?"

"It's going to be a while." She smiled reassuringly at Aaron, who hovered in the doorway, as if not sure whether to stay or run. "Quite a few hours, probably. Right now, I think it would be good for Susie to take a walk. Why don't you go with her?"

His Adam's apple bobbed. "But—what if the baby starts to come?"

"The baby won't come that suddenly. Trust me. Just let Susie stop walking and lean on you when a contraction occurs. You'll be fine."

He didn't look so sure, but he nodded and came to

take Susie's arm, hoisting her out of the chair. "We will walk, then."

She waited until they were out the door before setting about getting the room ready for the new little life who'd soon be taking up residence here. The familiar routine of laying out supplies and putting clean sheets and plastic—another gift from the birthing clinic—on the bed soothed away the last edges of strain.

Nolie was right. She was still a midwife, whether she had a building for her practice or not. She'd been paralyzed by the enormity of making decisions about her future, but here, with a baby on the way, she need only take the next step.

Thank You, Lord. Thank You for reminding me of who I am.

When she'd finished with the room, she went out to the porch to see how Susie was progressing with her walk. She found them coming slowly back to the house. A car was pulling out of the driveway—a police car.

She shielded her eyes against the red glow of the setting sun. "Was that Ted?"

Her heart gave an extra thump at the thought of him. He'd called every day during the past week, apparently accepting without comment Nolie's explanation that she didn't feel like talking yet.

In truth, she hadn't known what to say to him. She still didn't.

"Ja, Ted." Aaron rubbed Susie's back as another contraction started. "He heard that you were here and just wanted to be sure everything was all right."

He hadn't asked to see her, apparently. Well, that was to be expected. She understood that the bright promise of something between them was gone. And if she hadn't quite accepted it, she would. It would take time, maybe, to put away that dream, but she could do it.

She managed a smile as she helped Susie up the steps. "Everything is fine. I hope you told him that."

"Everything is fine." Fiona adjusted the flame on the oil lamp so that she could see a little better. She hadn't thought about how dark it would be in an Amish farmhouse in the middle of the night. "You're progressing just as you should."

"Ja, fine." Susie's mother, who'd arrived before Susie had gone into the second stage of labor, echoed the assurance. "First babies take some time to come."

Thank heaven Susie's mother was a sensible woman who took the birth of her grandchild in stride. Susie had gained strength from her presence.

Susie leaned back against Aaron, resting between contractions, her face pale. "I'm so tired. Too tired. I can't do it."

Fiona had heard that before, so often, and usually at just this stage. "You *can* do it. It's almost time to push. Your baby's about ready to be born."

Susie shook her head. "I can't. I can't." She was distracted, weary, losing the concentration she needed to get through the next few minutes.

"I know you're tired." Fiona kept her tone soft and soothing. "Don't think about that. Think about the happiness that's waiting for you. Think about having your baby in your arms." She leaned forward, holding Susie's gaze with hers. "That's worth fighting for, Susie. Isn't it?"

Slowly she nodded. "Ja. It is worth fighting for." She gripped Aaron's arms. "I am ready."

Chapter Sixteen

"You are beautiful. Yes, you are." Fiona crooned to the tiny baby boy and then settled him in the waiting arms of his mother.

"He is." Susie's plain face was beautiful, too, as she looked at her son.

Aaron leaned on the bed, watching his wife and newborn son with an expression of sheer wonderment on his face. "Our son. We have a son." It was as if he hadn't really believed it until this moment.

As often as Fiona experienced this moment, it never became old. Her heart swelled, and tears pricked her eyes. Always the birth of a new child was an affirmation of God's presence in their lives, a reminder that His miracles happened in just such everyday ways.

Susie's mother stood, tucking the quilt around her daughter. "The sun is already up. Time for a good breakfast for all of us."

She glanced at Fiona, and Fiona nodded, knowing what she meant. It was the right moment to leave the new little family alone together.

"That sounds like a great idea." She followed the older woman out of the room. "We can all use something to eat, and then maybe Susie can sleep for a bit."

"Ja." Susie's mother paused, looking at Fiona, her eyes soft behind the wire-rimmed glasses she wore. "You did good. Is good that you are come to us."

Fiona nodded, unable to speak for the lump in her throat. It *was* good that she had come here, to these people. Despite the trouble she'd encountered, even despite the loss of her house, she was at home here.

The decision she'd struggled with for the past week had already been made. She would stay in Crossroads. She didn't see her way clear yet, didn't have any idea how or where she would set up her practice again, but at least this much she knew—she was meant to be here.

She followed the woman into the kitchen, standing at the window to watch as the sun chased the shadows away. The sizzle of bacon in the pan reminded her of how long it had been since she'd eaten, but even without food, she felt energized. Strong. As if she could face whatever came and deal with it.

She hadn't been dealing with anything lately—not the loss of her house, not the situation with Ted. Instead she'd hidden, letting her family coddle and protect her.

The words she'd spoken to Susie came back to her. *Happiness is worth fighting for.* She'd been trying to encourage the tired young mother, but the words were true. And they applied to her, didn't they?

In the past week, she hadn't fought for anything. She'd withdrawn, just as she always did when faced with the risk of pain and rejection.

Understanding why she did that didn't make it right. She'd risked rejection when she'd approached the Flanagans, and she had a whole, loving family as a result. She'd risked again when she'd tried to mend the breach with her mother's family. She still wasn't sure how much the pain of Levi's arrest would affect them, but they'd stood by her while her house burned, and that was something.

Risk. Pain. Happiness. With every step toward belonging, there was a risk. There was a cost. Was she ready to face that?

Maybe the answer had been deep inside her all along. She had to face Ted once again. She had to risk hearing him say that it couldn't work between them. If he did, well, she'd live with that. But she wouldn't hide from the risk. Happiness was worth fighting for.

It was midmorning by the time Fiona arrived in Crossroads, having left the happy family enjoying their time together. She'd promised to check in on Susie in a few hours, but she had plenty of time to track down Ted.

Her stomach quivering with nerves, she approached Ted's office door. She opened it quickly, afraid that if she delayed for even a moment, she'd turn away.

The office was empty. She stood in the center of the small room, looking around. Odd that Ted would leave the door unlocked when he wasn't here, but maybe he figured Crossroads was safe again now that the vandals had been identified. Even the coffeepot was cold and empty.

She'd keyed herself up to face him, and now she was totally deflated. What should she do now? She turned to the door and there he was, hand on the knob.

She took a breath, trying to still the nerves that danced at the very sight of him. "Ted."

"Fiona, I thought you were still with Susie." He shoved his hat back on his head. "Is everything okay out there?"

"Just fine. They have a beautiful little boy." The memory curved her lips into a smile, easing her tension. "Susie is doing great."

"And Aaron? He didn't pass out on you, did he?"

They were actually smiling together, something she hadn't expected to see again. "He turned white a couple of times, but he held up beautifully. I'm sure he'll soon be bragging about it."

"I'll bet he will."

Silence fell between them. She couldn't seem to look away from him, but neither could she find the words she wanted to say.

"Ted, I—"

He stopped her with a quick shake of his head. "Look, before you say anything, there's something I want to show you. All right?"

She blinked, surprised. "All right."

"Good." He held the door open, ushering her out. "I'll drive. It's not far."

She slid into the front seat of the patrol car that waited at the curb and looked curiously at the array of gadgets on the dash. "I've never been in a police car before. I'm very impressed."

He smiled as he turned the ignition. "Don't be. This is pretty low-tech compared to most modern departments."

He pulled out into the street. Crossroads was never busy, but today it seemed more deserted than usual. Only one car was parked in front of the café, and even the post office didn't appear to be doing any business.

"Where is everyone?" She glanced back along the street.

"Guess they're all busy." He tried to say it casually, but there was suppressed emotion in his voice that drew her attention.

"Is something happening that I should know about?"

He shot her a glance she couldn't read. "Could be. Just be patient a second, and then you can tell me."

He rounded the corner. Ruth's general store appeared, looking none the worse for wear since the fire. Fiona's stomach tightened. In an instant she'd see the place where her home had been. She couldn't do this—

Her breath caught. She closed her eyes for a second, then opened them again. No, she wasn't dreaming. Where there had been a mass of smoldering ashes and charred timbers, raw new wood framed in a building that appeared like a ghost of what had once been there.

No, not a ghost. This was real.

People swarmed over the structure, some Amish, some dressed in jeans and sweatshirts. Hammers pounded and saws churned. Amish buggies stood next to dusty pickups and shiny SUVs. A long table laden with coffee urns and what looked like platters of food was set up next to Ruth's store.

"What…what's happening?" She leaned forward, one hand braced against the dash. "I don't…I don't understand." She looked at Ted, unable to take it in.

"What's to understand?" He shrugged, as if to dismiss this as something quite ordinary. "If a barn burns, the Amish will replace it in a day. Now, your house is going to take a little longer, since you won't be content with stalls, but then, we've got quite a lot of help."

"I can't believe this." She fumbled with the door, until finally he reached across her and opened it, his big hand warm against hers.

"Believe it." His voice was a low rumble that set her nerves quivering. "It's real."

Quickly, as if afraid he'd gotten too close, he slid out of the driver's seat, coming around the car to join her. People paused in their work when they saw her, raising a hand in welcome, and then turning back to the job at hand.

She glanced from one person to another, recognizing her Flanagan cousins working side by side with her Amish kin. That was why Nolie had been trying so hard to get her to Crossroads, obviously. She'd known all about it.

Her heart caught. Levi was there, working next to his father, his face solemn and intent.

"Levi—" Her voice choked as she remembered what had happened the last time she'd asked Ted about the boy.

"He's doing all right," Ted said quickly. He didn't look at her, and she wondered if he was remembering that, too. "He came clean with his parents and the church about everything that happened, and he accepted the punishment they meted out. I expect he's learned enough from this experience to last him a good long time."

It was a relief to know that Levi was right with his community, but that wasn't everything. "What about the court? Did he get a lawyer?" Siobhan's promise to find an attorney for Levi had been swamped by everything else that happened.

Ted nodded. "He has representation, and the other boys admitted he just acted as a lookout on a couple of their pranks. He refused to go the nights they tried to torch the barns—maybe he'd figured out by then that he was in too deep."

"Will the court see it that way?" She was looking to Ted for answers again.

"He'll get off with probation. The other two will get community service, I imagine."

"Two?" She looked at him, confused. "There were three, weren't there?"

"Yes, three." His voice sounded grim. "Our friend Jared isn't going to get off so lightly." His hand closed over hers, as if he thought she needed some support. "Jared torched your house."

She could only stare at him, amazed that she hadn't even wondered until this moment how the fire had started. "Are you sure?"

He nodded. "We were already on his trail when his parents brought him in. They'd found the evidence. To do them credit, they were appalled. Maybe they'll finally face the truth about that kid."

Surprisingly, there was little anger in her heart when she thought of the boy. *I forgive him, Father. Help me when I feel resentment or anger toward him.*

"Come on." Ted tugged at her hand. "See what you think of your new home and office." He drew her toward the building, holding her steady while she walked up a plank that led to the first floor. "Mose had a lot of good ideas after working on the renovation. We thought you could use a waiting room that's a little larger, seeing as how you'll probably have a lot of new clients in the next few years."

She stood next to him in what would be her waiting room, her throat tightening. "You've thought of everything, haven't you?"

But that wasn't what her heart was saying. *What about us, Ted? You've taken care of everything else, but what about what went wrong between us?*

As if he felt her thoughts, Ted's grip on her hand grew stronger. He nodded toward the Amish man working nearby, and she realized it was his brother.

"You know, every once in a while, my big brother Jacob thinks he has to straighten me out about things." He sounded casual, but she sensed the undertone of emotion in the words. "Seems like he felt compelled to tell me that a man had to be a blockhead to turn away from the woman he cared about because she acted out of the warmth of her heart to save another person pain."

Her heart was thudding so loudly she could hear it. "Do you listen when your big brother gives you advice?"

"Not always." He swung to face her more fully, clasping both her hands in his. "But sometimes, like now, he's right." The warmth from his hands flowed through her, unlocking the emotions that had been frozen for days. "I guess you know why I acted the way I did. Does knowing that mean you can understand and forgive me?"

She did know. He'd used the trust issue as a barrier between them, caught as he was between his own need to protect his community and fulfilling the law.

Her fingers moved on his. "You're not betraying anyone by doing the work God called you to, you know." She kept her voice soft, even knowing no one could hear them over the clatter of work going on around them.

"I know that now."

"I'm glad."

Ted's blue eyes seemed to have a flame deep inside them when he looked at her. "And I know it's not wrong to love the woman God brought into my life, either," he said softly. He drew her closer, until anyone who looked at them could guess what was happening between them. "Some people might say I'm a little old to go sweethearting again, but I'll risk it if you will."

Risk. There it was again. She understood now. She didn't get the reward without being willing to risk everything, in faith and in life.

She took the step that separated them, feeling his arms close around her, feeling the warmth of friends, family, community supporting them.

She was home. God had truly brought her home.

* * * * *

Turn the page for a sneak preview of
A SOLDIER'S HEART,
the next book in
The Flanagans series
by Marta Perry.

She was keeping an appointment with a new client, not revisiting a high school crush. Mary Kate Donnelly opened her car door, grabbed the bag that held the physical therapy assessment forms, and tried to still the butterflies that seemed to be doing the polka in her midsection.

What were the odds that her first client for the Suffolk Physical Therapy Clinic would be Luke Marino, newly released from the Army hospital where he'd been treated since his injury in Iraq? And would their short-lived romance in the misty past make this easier or harder? She didn't know.

She smoothed down her navy pants and straightened the white polo shirt that bore the SPTC letters on the pocket. As warm as this April had been, she hadn't brought the matching navy cardigan. The outfit looked new because it was new—just as new as she was.

Nonsense. She lectured herself as she walked toward the front stoop of the Craftsman-style bungalow. She was a fully qualified therapist, and just because she'd chosen to concentrate on marriage and children instead of a career didn't make her less ready to help patients.

The grief that was never far away brushed her mind, and she pushed it aside. Neither she nor Kenny had imagined a situation in which she'd be raising their two young children alone, but life and death were unpredictable.

For Luke, too. He probably hadn't imagined a situation in which he'd be coming back to his mother's house with his legs shattered from a shell and nerve damage so severe it was questionable whether he'd walk normally again.

Ruth Marino's magnolia tree bloomed in the corner of the yard, perfuming the air, even though Ruth herself had been gone for nearly a year. Luke had returned from Iraq for the funeral. Mary Kate had seen him standing tall and severe in his dress uniform at the church. They hadn't talked—just a quick murmur of sympathy, the touch of a handshake—that was all.

Now Luke was back, living in the house alone. She pressed the button beside the red front door. Ruth had always planted pots of flowers on either side of the door, pansies in early spring, geraniums once the danger of frost was past. The pots stood empty and forlorn now.

There was no answering sound from inside. She pressed the button again, hearing the bell chime echoing within. Still nothing.

A faint uneasiness touched her. It was hardly likely that Luke would have gone out. Rumor had it that he hadn't left the house since he'd arrived, fresh from the Army hospital. That was one reason why she was here.

"You went to high school with him." Carl Dickson, the PT center's director, had frowned at the file in front of him before giving Mary Kate a doubtful look. "Maybe you'll have better luck than anyone else has getting him in here for an assessment. He's refused every therapist we've sent. You certainly can't do any worse."

She had read between the lines on that. She was new and part-time, so her time was less valuable. Dickson didn't want to waste staff on a patient who wouldn't cooperate, but he also didn't want to lose the contract from the US Army if he could help it.

She pressed the bell again and then rapped on the door, the uneasiness deepening to apprehension. What if Luke had fallen? His determination to reject every professional approach, even every act of kindness, left him alone and vulnerable. If he'd fallen…

She grabbed the knob, but it refused to turn under the pressure of her hand. Kicking the door wouldn't help her get in, tempting as it was, and it certainly wouldn't help Luke if he lay helpless inside.

Quickly she stepped from the stoop and hurried around the side of the house. Maybe she could get in the back door. The way was familiar enough, since Ruth had changed little or nothing over the years.

Mary Kate had grown up less than two blocks away, in the house where her parents still lived. Her brothers had been in and out of Luke's house constantly in those days, as he'd been at their house, shooting hoops on the improvised driveway court. A frayed basket still hung forlornly from the Marino garage.

The back porch had the usual accumulation of things—a forgotten rake, a trash can, a couple of lawn chairs leaning against the wall. She hurried to the door and peered through the glass at the kitchen.

At first she thought the figure in the wheelchair was asleep, but Luke roused at her movement. His head came up, and he fastened a dark glare at her. He spun the wheels of the chair, but she didn't think he was heading for the door to welcome her in. Before he could reach it, she opened the door and stepped inside, closing it behind her.

"Don't you wait to be invited?" The words came out in a rough baritone snarl. Luke spun the chair away from her, as if he didn't want to look at her.

Or, more likely, he didn't want her to look at him.

Her throat muscles convulsed, and she knew she couldn't speak in a normal way until she'd gotten control of herself. But Luke—

The Luke she remembered, as a high school football hero, as a police officer, as a soldier when his reserve unit was called up, had been all strength and muscle, with the athletic grace and speed of a cheetah. Not this crumpled, pale, unshaven creature with so much anger radiating from him that it was almost palpable.

She set her bag carefully on the Formica and chrome table, buying a few more seconds. She glanced around the kitchen. White painted cabinets, linoleum on the floor, Cape Cod curtains on the windows—no, Ruth hadn't changed anything in years.

"I didn't think I had to stand on ceremony with an old friend," she managed to say, her voice gaining strength as she spoke. "Besides, I had a feeling you might not let me in if I waited for an invitation."

He didn't answer the smile she attempted, sparing her only a quick glance before averting his face. "I don't want company, Mary Kate. You must have heard by now that I've made enemies of half the old ladies at church by rejecting their casseroles."

"Mom wouldn't appreciate being called an old lady, so you'd better not repeat that in her hearing."

Her mother had tried, and failed, in her quest to see that Luke had a home-cooked meal delivered by the church every night. Luke had apparently slammed the door in the face of the first volunteer and then refused to answer the bell for anyone else. After a week of refusals, her volunteers had given up.

"I didn't mean—" He began, and then stopped, but for just an instant she'd seen a glimmer of the old Luke before his face tightened. "I don't want visitors."

"Fine." She had to make her voice brisk, or else the pain and pity she felt might come through. That would only make things worse—she knew that instinctively. "I'm not here as a visitor. I'm here as a physical therapist."

He stared for a moment at the crest on her shirt

pocket, swiveling the chair toward her. His legs, in navy sweatpants, were lax against the support of the chair.

"Doesn't your clinic have rules against you barging in without an invitation?"

"Probably." Definitely, and as the newest member of the staff, she couldn't afford to break any of the rules. On the other hand, she couldn't go back and admit failure, either. "Are you going to report me, Luke?"

Dear Reader,

Thank you for picking up this newest book in the story of the Flanagan family. I hope you enjoyed visiting old friends and meeting new ones.

It was a tricky business to introduce a previously unknown cousin to the Flanagans in this story, but I hope you'll feel it worked. In this case, the story came first—I knew I wanted to write about the Amish in Pennsylvania, so I needed a heroine, such as Fiona, who had a very good reason for being there and struggling for acceptance. And the character of Ted, with his need to create a life between two worlds, really touched my heart.

I owe profound thanks to my friend Winona Cochran, professor of psychology as well as a nurse-midwife with experience in the Amish community, for her invaluable contributions to *Restless Hearts*.

I hope you'll let me know how you felt about this story. I'd love to hear from you, and you can write to me at Steeple Hill Books, 233 Broadway, Suite 1001, New York, NY 10279, e-mail me at marta@martaperry.com, or visit me on the Web at www.martaperry.com. Please come back for the next Flanagan story, *A Soldier's Heart,* coming in May 2007.

Blessings,

Marta Perry

QUESTIONS FOR DISCUSSION

1. What qualities in Fiona make her a good nurse-midwife? Do you think she could be as effective without those innate qualities?

2. Ted struggles every day with the inherent conflict between his upbringing and his calling to be a policeman. Do you sympathize with his need to succeed? Do you feel he makes the right decisions in balancing that conflict?

3. Fiona reacts to the problems of her childhood by avoiding emotional risk. Were you able to sympathize with her attitude, even if you didn't approve of it? Why or why not?

4. Ted wants to protect his friends from the trouble he feels would come with Fiona's presence. Have you ever had similar feelings of longing to protect a friend?

5. Nolie tells Fiona that she feels God has brought her to Crossroads, and that thought is echoed by several other characters. Have you ever felt that God has led you to a particular place or situation?

6. Fiona's acceptance in the community comes when people see the depth of her caring for others. How do newcomers become accepted in your community?

7. Ted quotes the story of Joseph in the Old Testament when he tries to explain how God has worked in his life. Have you ever had an experience in which God brought good out of a situation where another person intended harm?

8. Fiona sees the similarity between the message Ted takes to heart and her own special verse, but she struggles to see how God is working for good in the troubles that come to her. Have you ever faced that same struggle?

9. "Happiness is worth fighting for," Fiona tells Susie as she encourages her through the birth of her child. But she has to learn for herself that happiness only comes when she is willing to risk the pain of rejection. Do you think she does the right thing?

10. The Amish are a unique group in contemporary American culture. What things do you find to admire in their lifestyle? What things do you disagree with? Why?